THE SMILE OF THE SIBYL

BOOK I OF THE INSPECTOR QUEBERON MYSTERIES

JOANNA PATERSON

SIBYL PRESS

Illustration by Joanna Paterson.

Published by Sibyl Press. *It seemed to her she was making friends at last—ones that carried the wisdom of the past into the present.*

www.sibylpress.com

ALSO BY JOANNA PATERSON

Every crime novel has to have its criminal characters and these are inventions! None of them reflect actual human persons. Only the ghosts are not fictional—they reflect archival investigation and many hours spent in archives and libraries reading history and diaries. The historical figures are therefore real people. The landscape gardens can be seen today and I enjoyed staying there and walking amongst the temples and lakes and the many ornaments and memorials of times past.

May you enjoy each fictional character and each aspect of the Dessau landscape gardens. I hope you too will come to treasure them.

CONTENTS

PROLOGUE

"I'll be dead. These dark rocks squeeze words and thoughts into silence. They win. He wins. The Direktor has clanked the door shut. Archaeologists, strangers, will uncover my skeleton, my remains." And she cried, and sobbed, and no-one heard. Elizabeth was in a dank prison, in a forgotten castle, and she was locked in. It seemed to her to be forever.

No-one knew where she was. No-one *would* find her.

In this black nemesis of a dungeon she longed for those outside. They were free. Her erstwhile companions walked by. And even the ghosts were free. She was cut off by the thick, impenetrable walls of Coswig Castle. This mad castle was just beyond the landscape garden of Dessau-Woerlitz, just beyond the bend of the River Elbe.

Not least she longed for the comfort of her ghostly friends, those she held dear from the past. These ghosts brought the legacy of friendship from woman to woman as the gift of history. And this was important to her. She had unearthed it as she worked in the archive. All this seemed lost now, as darkness set in.

THE ISLE OF MULL

Elizabeth Hammerstein looked out at the ravishing blue of the Firth of Lorne and the double-horned peak of Cruachan. The colours on water and land were never the same. In the distance the balled fist of Duart Castle was raised over the bay. The scene was agitated but beautiful. She especially liked the rushing sound of the ocean waters and the wild heights of the land.

And, like the waters, she was restless.

She surveyed the far trees, just in leaf, and the slope to the sea. She bent forwards to see down the lawns of the estate, edged with the balustrade and the well-placed stone garden buildings. Her sightline followed the path to wider, extended lawns and to the lighthouse. The seas met here, the Lorne and Mull Sounds uniting, and she could see the turbulent waves overlapping.

She paused, torn in two directions. One was the easy way out: to turn her back on her desire for uncovering women's history and remain on Mull; to sail and to garden and to let things be as they are. The other option was to keep searching for what she found that made a difference and would matter, especially for friendship among women. Was the past significant for the present?

Elizabeth was troubled. She had her hunches. But she would have to journey to foreign lands. She surmised in the eighteenth century there were international links and models for friendship. But she couldn't be sure of what was coming.

Elizabeth wore bright wool stockings, a nice brown short skirt, and a red pullover against the chill wind. She was used to the cold in Scotland which most would describe as wintry, were they not accustomed to what meant spring on the island. Snowdrops showed and the daffodils speared green shoots through the ground. Only the hills remained white.

In her younger days, she and her half-sister had taken the ferry to school. They had journeyed from Craignure to Oban. They pulled funny faces at each other under colourful umbrellas even when the ferry was grey with rain. Bright and unusual umbrellas were the name of the game. Of course, there were brilliant days as well when they chased each other on deck. Until, that is, Mhairi had gone all shy and waved her diamond engagement ring.

Elizabeth whiled away the time, left to herself, after that. Until, that is, she suddenly became interested in history and what it told her. She discovered that personal events, even of long ago, influenced her decision-making.

Although these characters dressed in bodices and skirts or the funny knee-length trousers of men of past times, their joys and woes were important to her. She wanted to explore them. They reached all the way into her own life.

"Women did marvellous, exceptional things. Even when I read about them living long ago, even if they are now ghosts, I feel them beckon. The past has modern questions, inventions conceived long ago that might matter today. And I want to be involved."

Elizabeth hummed a lovely tune to herself. "I want to make friends like they did. I want life, liberty, and freedom." She denied complications and loneliness, the deaths, hanging and imprisonment, even the witch trials that deeply marked the past; she wanted exemplary womanly models she could use. And she was trying for international recognition.

As she engaged in searching the past, she followed meaningful lives. The lives, as some would have it, of ghosts.

MAKING UP HER MIND

Elizabeth leaned over the parapet. Her home behind her turned its blank windows in her direction. She was still fundamentally undecided. She could risk oblivion examining old papers, lives of forgotten women who lived centuries ago.

She had grown up here; bounced down the lawns as a child; become erudite. She was no longer in her teens, but a grown woman, and ready to sacrifice her comfort, willing to let history unsettle her.

Elizabeth loved the Enlightenment. Hallowed ground for giant strides. Waking up to equality—friendship a new order of the day. Men and women! And they tried to practice it; at first so tentative and then leaping forward. Could she search out the truth? Or would she meet the stone wall that was so grave-like, so silent, because no one wanted gender issues flaming up?

Her mouth curved into a smile, very pleasing, and the rest of her dressed in fashionable clothes, as a girl she had been taught to be winsome and please her elders. But now was the time to throw niceness aside, to blow embers into bright flames. She was lighting the torch.

She turned. The stone house with its turrets and crow-steps was there facing her. The ever-alive tossing sea with its channels and tides was before her. This was her inspiration. She decried safety, suddenly and completely.

Mhairi came to join her.

Her half-sister wanted laurels for her competent management of the estate. "Elizabeth, since this is where you'll be settling, how about doing some renovating that is pleasing to us both? You might even try planning out the new garden."

Overbearing as ever, thought Elizabeth. I cannot. I cannot do this.

She turned once more. She saw the ocean in ebb and flow. The unpredictability of weather was there. The power of rushing water and stormy winds just where the Sounds and the bays and the inlets met were forevermore tossing in her mind; she made her decision, then and there. The ocean world had laws of its own and she would brave it on *terra incognita*. These natural forces took hold of her; she would resist, but in the end be glad of danger.

"No," Elizabeth said, "I will not stay. I have miles to go before I sleep, as they say. I can't settle down. I want to investigate that troublesome corner of history called female friendship. The eighteenth century started putting it on the map. It seems to me no-one pays enough attention to this. Women started it. Men liked it. I need to investigate internationally. Not that it will do me any good!"

Elizabeth had recently been elevated to the position of professor for her studies of the Enlightenment. But despite attaining such a high honour, she lacked support. She was one of the few women in a commanding role. And she was isolated.

"I'm keen on new visions. The Enlightenment contained so many novelties. But I'll go abroad. There," and she was convinced of it, "they'll have to grapple with me!" And she laughed, hoping her half-sister would understand.

"Can't I make you happy just being here? Can you be content with just plain idleness or take up a supervisory role? Just enjoying access to Oban and the island and the garden here, with its vistas? This is more than most are handed in a lifetime!"

Elizabeth's thoughts veered to Hugh.

Hugh was Elizabeth Hammerstein's one soft spot. She had grown up with him. She was like an older sister to him, although he was her nephew. She had enjoyed wild adventures with him; not romance but hefty jousting, revelry, and adventures. He was her junior by many years.

They had used the dinghy together and more than once ended up trailing wet feet and unruly hair up the sandy or rocky beaches of the Isle of Mull; or the muddy flatlands of wider bays.

He had trailed her to Glasgow University to pursue his own studies. Then she had lost sight of him.

GERMANY

Elizabeth's mind was made up to travel to Germany; not the prosperous West Germany, as it was then called, but the newly affiliated East. This was the part of Germany that was still struggling. She was going to find out if her new theories of the past about women of the Enlightenment had traction in that early liberal state of princely sovereignty, the one named Anhalt-Dessau. She had visited that country briefly once before; it was demanding.

What a contrast to Mull it would be, she thought, to be on the Continent and landlocked. Dessau was to the south and slightly to the east of Berlin, one of the first to preserve a landscape garden, as these new ventures were called.

She straightened, declaring: "I'm not domestic. I want to explore a nation new to me. I don't want to sit on my backside and be complacent, particularly when I'm about to advance into the unknown past. I have always wanted to investigate what happened. What were the consequences of freedom? What were the binding ties of new ways of thinking and new emotions?"

She surveyed the distant hills from her stance on the terrace. Glanced over the ever changing, lapping, turbulent, but oh so blue waters. She was becoming more like them. She was a questing soul. History was her mainstay, but the present was an uncertainty.

She wanted the hidden to come to the forefront. She was going to verify her commitment to lives so different and lively. And diaries of the past left unread.

Later Elizabeth strolled toward the sea, through the garden, between the statues that some ancestor had brought from Italy to grace the walk away from the house. The afternoon was already waning. The pale whiteness of statuary overrode the greens of the garden. And they were casting shadows. And she was entangled in them.

One of them, Apollo of the Muses, made her stumble on the path. Her foot twisted. She nearly knelt, but straightened at the last minute. Paying homage would not do. Instead she jutted out her chin and called on

Diana, patron of the hunt, the moon, and armed with bow and arrow. She repeated to herself that she was independent of mind.

Nonetheless she saw the shadows. Little was to be gained by pretending she was unfamiliar with the play of light. Never was there shape without its shadow. The islands rose from the sea. They cast their high hills on the incoming waves there. One could not be defined without the other.

Elizabeth became more resolute than ever. She would inhabit the archives and libraries of Dessau and the landscape gardens of Woerlitz and the Luisium.

She was drawn to the country house there that was dedicated to the quirky, often self-willed, but often seen in published literature as the oh-so-melancholy Louise, of eighteenth-century birth.

The Greeks and the Romans, so many of their gods and what they represented, were featured there too. Their republican values were revered and emulated in the past. This gave her traction when searching out a paradigm for the changing relations between the sexes. This might feed into her ideas. The ideal baited the real. It mattered to see why change was taking place in land-scape gardens; how the landscape gardens retained oh so quietly the revolutions of the past.

Elizabeth wanted to accentuate this, to bring the

unseen into view, giving credence to the belief of the ancients and of centuries long ago, casting them into the light from a different angle.

FIRST STEPS

Inspector Horatio Queberon kicked his car's tyres. It was more than a pastime. Venting his frustration at his lack of evidence to make his arrests, this was his way of showing he was still being professionally active. He was testing his ability to make his policeman's presence felt. The tyres gave a susurrating sigh.

With their heavy breathing, the tyres at least expressed submission. He acknowledged their noisy kindness. But he was surreptitiously seeing if he was as sober as he looked. He had just finished an extensive lunch with several glasses of fine wine. His tyre-kicking would challenge anybody with the wrong ideas. Anybody that is, who thought he was not entirely free of this lovely red wine.

Inspector Queberon had dined in lonely splendour and copiously. His special pleasure was beef steak with fries. He had eaten Angus ribeye and added glorious red Bolney wine—at least two glasses—the special British produce of vineyards from West Sussex. An unusual import, but very well worth drinking, he thought.

In emerging from the hotel car-park, he viewed the garden kingdom once more. He wanted to assess it in a new light. He was on a special case, one which mattered in the garden kingdom. And, he reflected, it also related to police business in Dessau. Drug trafficking was a new offence in these parts, in a region which had been mostly peaceful.

Woerlitz, the landscape garden, was being used to distribute illicit goods through its extensive waterways system.

Just now he was viewing it through a haze of culinary pleasures. Woerlitz surrounded him as did its myriad copies farther afield, and not just the landscape gardens. Each was slightly different and each anglophile. He had adopted such leanings himself.

Of course, the British had their own eccentricities, but he, as he imagined it, liked to stand out a little here in Germany. Especially through his colourful socks and the balance of a tell-tale tie, all chapter and verse in its Oxford Baliol origins. And he stood out. It made him a dapper man. Set him apart from the general herd.

He checked over what he knew. Firstly, there was the lake. Back-breaking work with a thousand shovels. Dug by hand centuries ago.

Shaped to conform to the 1767 first re-creation of an English landscape garden, the place told the mythical stories of gods and goddesses linked to the reigning house of Anhalt-Dessau. This was typical of eighteenth-century man-built landscapes.

He was as erudite as any tourist looking at the Greek or Roman myths anchored here, and duty would require nosing about in the landscape. He would learn more. He stopped sighing and smiled.

The landscape garden hid a mansion house, in this case a bit top-heavy. The palm house set high on top of the building dominated the main house. Did the criminals hide there? Perhaps they used the palm trees, out-of-place in such a cold climate, to obscure themselves as they scrutinized the terrain?

Inspector Queberon kicked the car's fourth, rear, tyre. The gardens were perfect no doubt, but he cast his narrowed eyes upon the lake. He wanted to know who dared cross its placid waters with a shallow speedboat or gondola, collecting and distributing hallucinatory and deathly substances. The culprit must have steely nerves to slide around in such intricate man-made water features.

He murmured more quietly to himself, "the many

fishermen provide perfect cover. The trafficker could claim he was one of them. That would explain why he was not local. All he had to say was that he was learning a trade."

Inspector Queberon meditated further on the many possibilities a criminal might enjoy in these parts. All a speedboat required in essence was to sneak up and down the canals. There were plenty of these. The garden kingdom of Woerlitz was based on canals. They were dug out of ground where the Elbe in previous years spread its tributaries.

Queberon had paid attention to his many history lessons and laid many an ignoramus in his grave. But, although the historians paid plaudits to this uncommon officer, his fellow policemen made merry about his head being swollen and crammed with the facts he cited. His head is large, they laughed in derisory fashion, but his feet are oh so small.

"The aristocrat and learned Architect Friedrich William von Erdmannsdorff raised his dykes against the mighty river and stopped its flooding the land. He had canals dug so his friends the other nobles could reach his architectural wonders easily by using exotic gondolas. Every inch of the landscape is accessible by boat. There you have it, my friends. And I know where to look." He said this defiantly to the watery landscape he surveyed.

Inspector Queberon contemplated Erdmansdorff's feat. The terrain was set up to be navigable in the extreme, allowing aristocratic access to the display of the temples, gods, monuments, and other miscellaneous features.

He looked out to the assembled gods, goddesses, temples and vales, and thought how at dusk when the park and its conifers and exotic deciduous trees were but murky presences, any inconspicuous shapes or wandering gondola or speedboat might create only shadows. Even if any of the guests, say from luxury hotels, strayed into the unlit, darkening park, they could not see clearly. Only those in the know could find their way.

He tried once more to imagine who would benefit. One of the men he had in mind was the pastry cook. Queberon had an inkling there was more to him than met the eye. But although specializing in cakes he was also generally renowned for his cooking skills. And he seemed to work hard at his trade.

New to these parts, Manfred Broadford, whose very physique suggested dark doings, was tall, well-built and smirking. He had previously inhabited Hamburg and Berlin. Now he was head cook at the Orangerie.

But one mustn't get carried away by dealings with the successful 'nouvelle cuisine', or however they called it, Inspector Queberon told himself. He was quite prejudiced in favour of copious meals instead of scant ones. He still preferred huge steaks to lean, sparse offerings served on huge plates.

Inspector Queberon liked his food. But come what may he also liked his Woerlitz. There were not that many 'English' landscape gardens preserved intact. And it was his business to catch whoever was using the canals for illicit trade not thought about by happy wanderers. To be a cook would be perfect cover.

Before getting into his car—he had after all, to all observers, been an ineffective dreamer staring at metal gleaming silver on his car in the sun—he straightened his clothes and hiked up his trousers, even tightening his belt. Although he liked being big enough to intimidate the slim.

As he got behind the wheel, he meditated on one more relevant fact.

There was this connection between the many canals and all was open to them, including the way to Hamburg. The Elbe mouth was at that great seaport. It was cosmopolitan and accessible. Anyone could traffic from there to here, or pick up the trade along the mighty river with its many boats. Or, indeed, its many speedboats.

BABYLONIA

Speculation was no proof. But the Inspector wanted his thinking to cover all eventualities. He moved on to other people on his radar. He had heard—by way of gossip, it has to be said—that a luxury hotel was planned. It needed official approval for building on site and the legitimacy of deeds to the land. Maybe there was a connection between this opulence and the money to be made by way of smuggling? Something in the impulse to marry money and land?

He drove toward the city.

Queberon had his ear to the ground. He had heard the luxury hotel would be themed on the landscape garden. What a theme park and its income brought its owners, he could not imagine.

. . .

"AN INSPECTOR BORDERING on the obese! He ought to tramp his paths by the police station more assiduously," thought the haughty Babylonia von Moritzburg maliciously, when she thought of Queberon at all.

She ducked in and out of the Grey House, one of the Woerlitz attractions. This House had been constructed for Louise von Anhalt-Dessau. She'd been the wife of Leopold Franz, the Prince, the one he'd left, without bothering to think he was being disloyal. How Louise dealt with this wasn't of interest to the attractive Babylonia. She vaunted her figure and red lipstick and had men so desirous of her that they crawled on the floor after her.

Louise was so equivocal a spirit to Babylonia that she despised her. Any modern woman, she thought, saw the advantages the female sex could command.

Louise had at first treasured her alliance with Franz, but this had darkened to revulsion. The Prince had revelled in his illegitimate liaison with the head gardener's daughter, Luise Schoch.

Babylonia was not interested in Louise. "But this Grey House, a haven for Louise von Anhalt-Dessau, has its merits!" she opined, "because it advertises the garden kingdom as a place in which to linger—and this provides tourists with places to investigate. They'll want a luxury hotel to stay in. And every attraction spells more money for me—and then I can do precisely what I want."

She already had some money through her divorce from the aristocrat Boris von Moritzburg. What she lacked was the legitimacy of land ownership. She grinned, sure of hiring an academic of suitable skills to unearth the title deeds from the archives of the Wissenschaftliche Bibliothek.

She chortled happily, with a spring in her step that made her curly hair bounce. And she wiggled her attractive hips lasciviously. And she added in her fluted, high notes because no-one present could hear her secret, "to find my inheritance in land deposition I engaged the outwardly placid-looking Wilhelm Paternoster. What a money-hungry academic he is, rot his bones."

Paternoster was not her cup of tea, but, hang it all, she thought, he would do, especially with his networks. He was intimately connected with the Preservation Society, of which Direktor Edwyn Eszett was in charge. She needed the approval of the vainglorious Direktor Edwyn Eszett for her luxury hotel.

Babylonia felt good about her plans. She knew she was next in line for lands adjacent to the dated showpiece Vesuvius. She only had to prove it.

This man-made volcano was a relic of Franz and Erdmanndorff's Grand Tour and stood its ground on the east side of the landscape gardens. Just behind it was a nice field of turnips. This was just the parcel of land Babylonia wished to inherit. Her luxury hotel would have an exotic view of that exotic replica volcano. And if she could have the Preservation Society light the volcano's fire, guests could revel in dramatic views of bright flames and black night.

Vesuvius was indeed a strange intrusion in a landscape garden, but she thought the black-tipped mountain worthy of the theme park she envisioned. Smoky fir branches were put in the cone of the Vesuvius and these mirrored fire and smoke in the lake. Smoke spiralled out of the cone into the night sky. Thus, fiery life came into its own by imitating the real thing. This fiery spectacle was a romantic reminder of how the real Vesuvius had erupted in the eighteenth century in the Bay of Naples.

Babylonia glanced at the replica volcano from her walk on the path by the lake. She would soon emerge again by the Grey House. She had left it by exiting out the garden gate, having taken this detour to please herself.

She fingered her keys to the main Mansion House, given her recently by Direktor Eszett, who was head-over-heels in love with her. More importantly, that is to her, he was susceptible to the idea of a hotel with thematic excursions all over Woerlitz. To have the head of the Preservation Society on your side was not bad going. Not that she was susceptible to Direktor Eszett's wooing; he was such a stuck-up exemplar of preservation. She much preferred the younger and more energetic Manfred, the handsome dark-haired chef. What a toy-boy!

Babylonia saw the tail end of an unmarked police car headed away from Woerlitz as she emerged onto the main street. She recognized the man at the wheel and saw the red tail-lights of Inspector Queberon's car.

CHANCE MEETINGS

J ust as Inspector Queberon's Mercedes was turning into the quieter reaches of Dessau, the stranger to these parts, Elizabeth Hammerstein, was deciding which tram to take.

She had jumped on an early bus and was walking past the middle of town where the spirited fountain splashed continuously over its bronze-coloured and tall-spiralled upward shape. The fountain lent a bright start to the morning.

Her aim was to collate and organize her notes despite the jiggles of the tram car which was soon to take her to the archive.

Elizabeth was wondering about the archivist, who in turn must be wondering about her. She thought the archivist brave, a woman among all the men, and investigated her on the internet. She surmised she was a natty dresser. Her reputation for clothes stylish but business-like had been quite evident. She wore suits and silk blouses. She discreetly wore her long hair in a bun.

Elizabeth hoped underneath all that sobriety the archivist was open to ideas of women forging friend-ships with their own kind—by way of linking the Enlightenment with advances toward our modern world—feminism, really.

She was on the way to the archive because she wanted to know more about Louise of Anhalt-Dessau. Here was a mystery, thought Elizabeth: An eighteenth-century woman of noble blood in exalted position who was unhappy and finding solace in her female friends. Louise felt drawn to Henriette von Lippe-Weisenfels, recently in Dessau because Prince Albert, brother to Franz, had negotiated their marriage. This jaunty and lively woman was married to Albert for strictly dynastic reasons.

How did these two find friendship? Elizabeth was unsure. She wanted to investigate, was prepared to let things fall into place and speak out about what happened. She was convinced that this was a friendship of consequence.

In the meantime, be it as it may. She would like to know more about Eva Delamotte, the archivist. She was certainly not as flashy as these trams. Here the tram came, it was turning a corner and ringing and clanging before it slid to a halt.

She got on, but she was still deep in thought. The refurbished water-tower, where the archive was located, remained some stops away, but her mind was on her investigations into the subtleties of centuries ago and what they meant for the present.

Elizabeth pondered her approach. The archivist will have to listen to whatever papers I would like to see. She'll have to help.

This would lead her to what could be extracted from papers lodged in the archive.

I want to know what brought Louise to misjudge so completely a tragic miscarriage and false pregnancy, she thought. And I want to know why Henriette's marriage ended in divorce.

But she was diverted as she looked out of the tram window. She saw an imposing person. This was the tall, well built, and handsome pastry cook, her next-door neighbour at her accommodation next to the former stable area of the Luisium, Manfred Broadford. He was walking with an academic she knew, Dr. Wilhelm Zaubertier. Both were deep in conversation. Elizabeth guessed it was about the conference to which she had been invited and which would be convened later that summer.

Zaubertier was aspiring to supplant an old professor

in Berlin. He was an academic climber to the top rungs of the ladder.

He would be biting Manfred Broadford's ear off about providing his renowned modern food and especially pastry for the conference goers and their audience. Hopefully there would be something good to eat. The cook was ambitious too.

The tram slid away. Elizabeth concentrated on her notebooks.

On Elizabeth's arrival, Eva Delamotte cast her shadow before her, as she usually did in the reception area. It heightened her authority.

Elizabeth was all attention. Delamotte emerged from behind the desk, collected and ever so cool. Eva Delamotte considered herself to be the epitome of efficient archivists.

WHAT ELIZABETH DIDN'T KNOW WAS the extent of subterfuge reigning in the archive. The pallid Paternoster was there ahead of her, his nose buried in reams of Louise's *Tagebuch*. Archive users were not supposed to know about each other, but this was too obvious. Paternoster was waving Louise's supposed hypochondria about and he was terrifically smug about it too. He sported a self-satisfied smile.

"You can't disprove how outrageous that bitch of a

consort was," he said. "She sucked Franz into an advantageous marriage and then wailed and miscarried."

He looked all around, triumphant. "The good pastor Reil, a contemporary, says so."

Paternoster played his card for all to see. He loved reactions—and he was sure to get them in others' outrage about his comments. On the other hand, he drew attention to his expertise. Remarkable people hired him. What most did not know was his serious side. He was a scholar of note, employed sometimes even by the Preservation Society. He let himself be hired for grand sums and used his knowledge to advantage. Paternoster was keen on power. He was well-trained but in essence mercenary.

Eva Delamotte did not bat an eye. She was used to all sorts—especially men denigrating women—very often met with even in modern times. But Elizabeth was new to her and a stranger from northern, Scottish climes. She briefly cast her eyes heavenward because of Paternoster then asked very civilly, "And what can I do for you?"

Paternoster winked at both of them. He did not take them seriously. Then he turned to Elizabeth and looked her up and down. He seemed little impressed by her stature and her sedate manner. He misjudged them both entirely. He thought them inconsequential.

He exited without another word, feeling superior.

NOTHING BUT PAPERWORK

The writers of the papers, these people which the historians were all seeking, turned to one another. They were now ghosts.

The meaning of papers rustling without a human hand turning them would have disturbed even the blustering Paternoster.

But the invisible ladies made a point of rustling. They rose of a piece, their long gowns catching only slightly on the thick paper of the *Tagebuch.* They held their heads together, then apart. What they said to each other became more distinct.

"Paternoster turned the pages so abruptly. I don't think he understands. We are bound to defend our way of life. Not to have it used for his purposes. We remain committed to one another and that is how we want to be interpreted."

Henriette spoke quietly, "I value what you did. Let us remain true to one another. We have come through so much. Let us value our experience."

Louise and she clasped ghostly hands. They slid gracefully out of the Landesarchiv and flew towards the Luisium. They were no more than shivers of light. But they showed purpose in their flitting in the direction of their home. And it was also the direction in which Woerlitz lay. They were going to see to their rights.

THEY SURVEYED the whole extensive landscape park in its various conceptions as princely grounds and went wherever they liked—and they floated high above, free of any inhibition. After all, they were ghostly inhabitants of the earth.

They both knew the Luisium well because they had resided there. In its empty rooms they gathered amongst the elite that were dead now in the flesh, but alive, and even more powerful, having slipped their mortal coils. "Just enough to have a soiree should we want to converse," said Henriette to Louise, "and entertainment with ghostly music on your lovely harpsichord."

Louise and Henriette wore, on occasion, gowns of silky white with sky-blue or moonlit yellow shawls.

Their eyes shimmered. Their long hair was combed nicely. Their shoes glinted in the dark.

Louise said, "I'm so glad we are so active in the shadowy dusk and the evocative glades of the night. And by daylight we sometimes even seem substantial. A good thing we have common goals."

They appraised the land.

Prince Albert had built the modest, but double-stair-cased castle of Kuhnau, now taken over by the head office of the Preservation Society.

The landscape gardens extended from the dykes and main neo-classical mansion of Woerlitz to Kuhnau by way of the Luisium and the Georgium. This latter building was the residence of Hans Georg, the brother after Franz. The Georgium extended to the Elbe River and boasted many additional lakes, man-made, but imitating the wild.

The Georgium also featured the ruined bridge that was visible from the very straight road that aimed at the Elbpavilion. This tower was oriented toward the sun and moon and the ghostly wanderers admired it.

The Elbpavilion, with its blossoming chestnut trees, was a landmark. The Luisium too was a cubical tower and was their safe haven, as ghosts could pass in and out through walls. Louise and Henriette cherished the glorious simplicity of floating into any place they wanted. The Luisium was an eighteenth-century house, but so modern it shone as a cube through trees that hugged and darkened its gentle moonlit-pale colouring during the day and during the night.

They both knew that Elizabeth Hammerstein lodged near the Luisium in the Eyserbeck House, an easy walk onto the knoll harbouring where they most liked to be. They were keen to perceive what she would do to redress their grievances and bring to life more vividly the repression and misunderstanding they had endured in life—and, not least, through long historical neglect.

GHOSTS

Louise and Henriette were out to avenge the callous disregard dealt out to them. Hardly ever were they seen in the light of their steely resolve. In the flesh they had both separated from their spouses. Their miscarriages and a false pregnancy had united them and paved the way for a friendship which proved eternal.

They had been charmed into noble but useless lives. The promises held out to them had failed to materialise in any significant form. When they became anxious as pregnant women, no spouse helped them. Desolation about their children, as yet unborn, entered their plunging emotions. They found solace in supporting each other.

Now, dead as they were, they could do what they

liked. Life, arduous as it was, had united them. And in the afterlife they drew together as ghosts. Above all, they could roam everywhere now and scare the daylights out of the living.

They liked their home ground, the landscape garden that was—perhaps in name only—built with Louise in mind. On a grander scale, Prince Franz von Anhalt-Dessau was using his many newly styled landscape gardens to engage with ideas of British Liberty, including the gardens of the Luisium. It emphasized independence of every domain in Franz's hands, no matter what his loyalties.

The avowed misogynist Eszett was their particular target. He simply did not think women had a mind, much less a mind of their own. He enjoyed his position and exercised his power. Above all, he was arrogant. His dislike of women was currently centred, so they suspected, on the scholar Elizabeth Hammerstein.

If Eszett was reprehensible, they hoped for better things from Elizabeth. They wanted to alter the present as all ghosts do.

Louise von Anhalt-Dessau wore good leather shoes with swirls at the heels. It was a symbol, that spiral; it was upward motion, it meant aspiring to higher things. She wanted responsibility. Whoever noticed, even in a shocked ephemeral glimpse of the seemingly "nothing", of a ghost, realized the apparition loomed purposely.

Both women wanted an historian like Elizabeth Hammerstein to do them justice. Henriette lingered on each elevation of the stairs of the Luisium as if her rising upwards were taking her inside herself. She had shut the portal with its dolphin knobs with a click. The thought she was pursuing leapt ahead of her. It concerned the relationship of past to present.

If enough existed in letters, journals, or objects, a life could be reconstructed. Henriette was seeing to that.

ELIZABETH HAD TAKEN much trouble here and at home to read about the women of the eighteenth century. She rehearsed her words to the archivist, hoping for sympathy.

"This is where liberation starts. Everyone in the enlightened eighteenth century savoured change. Every Duke and landowner tried consciously reconstructing Greek and Roman republicanism and democracy. Just look at those many temples in the landscape gardens! But there was more to it than that."

She talked up her convictions and what she was looking for. "Friendship among women is thrown in the face of feudalism. And the old mastery of men over women is diminished as a powerful force. Women choose women to confide in. They make the Grand Tour not just a male enterprise. Women started travelling by themselves. And both sexes cast an aura of modernism, of striving for expression."

As Elizabeth strove to impress the archivist, she warmed with enthusiasm to her theme. "Take Friederike Brun, for example, who shared a boat journey with Louise in Woerlitz and knew of Henriette. Friederike went off to Rome with Louise. Without men. They were trying for liberty.

"They were writing their journals. And centuries later they were read. Slowly, the words of Louise and Henritte found readers. Until then, they were preserved by archivists."

Dr. Delamotte struck Elizabeth as independent and modern. All the same, she came across as inscrutable.

Elizabeth looked at her covertly. But in front of the archivist she was quiet. Her cardboard box containing the papers and books she was consulting was being readied at the reception counter.

Elizebeth took the *Tagebuch* of Louise von Anhalt-Dessau and disappeared through the reading-room doors. She angled Louise's *Tagebuch* towards her and turned to an entry about Henriette.

THE DRUG TRADE

The light played wildly among the tattered clouds. It was visible above the heads of those bowed low to read the old-fashioned script in archives. But only those toting shallow speedboats over ground to hide them in convenient bushes sweated.

An unknown young man swore. He thought a gondola well worth grounding among the reeds instead. It would be simpler than manipulating a speedboat. But he would have to await dusk in either case. He settled himself in the sunny grasses.

He had hidden the shallow speedboat in the shrubbery the low willows made. He would use the speedboat eventually to make his get-away. It would be through the backwater of one of the canals.

He thought he might as well enjoy the day. The

speedboat, he thought, was well concealed. He must convince Manfred the gondola would carry the drugs he wanted better and with the ease of such a quiet and sturdy boat. If they deposited the innocuous bag with the drugs under the seat in an anonymous tool-box, this could make the gondola especially convenient.

What mattered was to study the weighty oars of the gondola. There might be some trickery involved with that. The regular gondoliers were not brawny by chance; they had earned their muscular bodies. Still, there might be something to be learned through the gondolier's actions especially in their adroit way of rowing, seated backwards, with those two heavy-weight oars manipulated by their fore-arms.

He contemplated a moment longer. But before he had finished his thoughts, drowsiness overtook him, and the scooting clouds ran overhead, making his existence wonderfully easy through oblivious sleep.

He was a native of Hamburg, not used to the humidity. He was a bit out of his depth on the winding River Elbe. His name was Hans.

His co-conspirator in crime, Manfred, was congratulating himself. He had successfully combined a chef's career with what he believed no-one could possibly suspect him of doing, his copious supply of drugs to those who frequented his restaurant. His was distribution in a very profitable manner.

He had recently given up a restaurant in Berlin. He could both ply his secret trade and be the master cook to some very discrete clients in the Orangerie. The restaurant with a summer terrace stood among the trees in the grounds of the Luisium. It had now become his restaurant; he was the manager. And he had even found that the left side of the Eyserbeck House was empty. He rented that long unoccupied extension, and renovated it himself, mainly in black and white as befits an acknowledged master cook and pastry chef. He celebrated with a few chosen friends and introduced his two cats, Old Fritz and Clausewitz.

The two cats liked the seclusion and the courtyard. They played their games. The Mulde River was close by, running as it did into the Elbe. It did not take him much calculation to be happy with a speedboat that was able to nose from waterway to waterway. Thank the lucky stars it was so simple. The currents were unfavourable, but that kept tourists out of the waters. And with himself stripped to the waist, enjoying his manly chest of curly black hair, he seemed like just another resident enchanted by the river landscape. He had found a young man to help, too.

THE GONDOLA OF DEATH

The sun was setting over the floodplains of the Elbe River. Darkness and light were juxtaposed. On the shore of the lake in Woerlitz were revealed monuments and ornaments from another time. Temples and graceful bridges rose between trees. But now shadows crept in, changing fine detail to a blurred chiaroscuro.

Slipping under the Palladian arches of the stone bridge, one of the gondolas normally used for sightseeing nosed out into the main body of the lake from one of the canals. The gondola was only a smudge with upward tilted prow. Its oars flicked occasionally, like a dragonfly settling on a curved blade of grass. It was certainly out of place. The other gondolas were safely chained to the pontoons. There they swung quietly, empty of their usual load of chattering tourists.

Walking along the path by the same lake, on its shore, Elizabeth Hammerstein turned to her companion. "As I was saying, what we see," she gestured towards the lake, "is thought-out design. All is solitude as if it were a stage, the grandeur and the beauty. The temples in the far distance suggest we are walking in the lands of the gods.

"The trees are gathered in groups; the delicate leaves, like talkative children, gather against the tall dark firs. Look at the dipping branches of the catalpa tree over there, a great dizzy waterfall of wavering, heart-shaped leaves and black shoots. Nature parades its groves and its cool, grassy lawns as if we were in paradise."

She paused. She was truly taken by the planting of the deciduous trees against the sombre firs. The dusk gathered pools of shadow; they made the landscape barely discernible. Helen followed her gaze.

Elizabeth added: "The design makes your eyes shift from darkness to light and back for the pleasure of it. Only the departed souls are meant to share this serenity, to make this a place for reading and writing poetry. Like Aeneas in Virgil's epic poem, we tread the edge of the lake in Avernus to commune with the Sibyl. She told him to seek out the dead for advice. Virtue, she said, is always undaunted."

Elizabeth stopped in appreciation. Her newly made acquaintance, the young Helen Brecht, stood with her admiring the dark blue lake and the dark, but varied trees. They especially liked the ancient leaning trees with the last golden tint of sunset.

As Helen stood next to Elizabeth, her eye caught the crooked black hook of the gondola's prow. The oars no longer dipped but trailed through the water. Being local she knew that the gondolas of the landscape park were heavy boats, very hard to steer. She saw it collide abruptly with the nearest bank, spoiling the picture. Then a spidery figure seemed to leap out and the gondola was pushed away, ripples agitating the water.

Both women watched the gondola drift.

"Unusual for anyone to be out so late," remarked Helen to Elizabeth. The sun was setting and the land was darker than the sky. The park had no artificial lighting and the car park was a longish walk beyond the trees. They would have to hurry if they were not to stumble on the gravel paths.

Elizabeth was reluctant to leave, despite the oncoming darkness. She turned once more to look back along the lake north-eastwards. "Take one last look at the Nymphaeum rising pale white with its Grecian columns and with its vineyards along the side. The white body of the water nymph over the lake near the *Schloss* … illusion and its properties … a lovely seduction …" She was enthralled to be part of this theatre of dusk.

Her voice trailed off. Helen saw the shimmering columns of the temple's reflection. Her gaze travelled over the lake and then back, then caught, hooked like a cast line, on the black half-moon of the gondola. Beside it she thought she saw something afloat, something very indistinct. A flapping motion. Then nothing. An illusion of shapes, a long shadow imprinted by a cat's paw of the evening breeze on the water. But maybe the figure casting off the gondola had returned? Maybe the figure had slipped and flailed in the water? Maybe the figure drowned?

They quickened their steps, disregarding what seemed only shadows. The park was silent; night was at their heels.

To reach the car park they had to turn towards the country house on their left. This was the famous Woerlitz mansion house built in the 1760s by the then reigning Prince.

Helen knew the Prince was anglophile and his admiration for Great Britain extended to the new landscape gardens. He built his own to show how much he liked what he saw in Great Britain. He travelled when this was an arduous pastime. He visited landscape gardens on the Thames and in Stourhead in Wiltshire and at Stowe in Buckinghamshire.

Helen was more knowledgeable than most; she offered the elder Elizabeth what came from being local and growing up here, but also from the talks she had attended. She wanted this Scottish lady—she could tell by the plaid skirt—to share her insight.

The Prince's Palladian house was light on its feet, appropriate to its fine geometric proportions, and fronted with tall Corinthian columns, aloof and lit by floodlights. But every window was now dark. Even from the highest windows the park was hidden in darkness.

They left the landscape garden to its unlit mystery. Nothing was strong enough to rise out of the darkness.

ACCIDENT PRONE

Helen was driving slowly. The headlights picked out the narrow country road and its tight curves. She had offered Elizabeth a ride home.

"So glad you don't want to join the immortals in the Elysian Fields," quipped Elizabeth. She was as yet untouched by anything but the glories of the garden they were leaving behind. She hardly focussed on the road in front of them.

The oak trees stood like palisades in the dark. It took all Helen's skill to steer smoothly and stay on the narrow tarmac lined by cats' eyes, their blinking pinpricks writhing with the road.

The sirens seemed far off. Elizabeth thought the whine seemed like a cat defending territory, his back fur standing on end. The yowling insistence echoed in her mind, and, clairvoyant, Helen picked it up, saying, "the sirens are like tomcats screeching on the back fence— the exact antithesis of walking in paradisiacal tran- quillity."

Helen had actually only known Elizabeth for the duration of their walk, a serendipitous encounter between the Pantheon and the Temple of Venus having started them talking. Elizabeth had stumbled down- wards and Helen had caught her as she was falling. Eliz- abeth had thanked her and enthused about Woerlitz. Helen had immediately taken to Elizabeth's obvious erudition; they were birds of a feather.

So Helen invoked the Elysian Fields, the other- worldly meadows and orchards alluded to in classical literature. "You and I, Elizabeth, are just the risen dead, women with books in our hands, libraries in our heads, painted into the landscape, walking the edges of old pictures, out of place when police cars and ambulances scream past."

Helen was steering the car over the flyover on the road between Woerlitz and Waldersee where it bridged the motorway. "Berlin to Munich in five hours," she said. "No parliament has ever been able to pass a law to limit the predatory desire of the power mad to bear down on lesser cars, slower drivers, people who think of cars only as transport."

Below them, leering red tail-lights and jousting high-beamed headlights cut through the night like scalpels. A game of chance, playing the dice late into the night, was right here.

"The Styx lit in lurid car-engine neon," remarked Elizabeth, appreciative of sceptical young women. They learned to drive, but didn't feel cars were their powerful and young equivalent. They preferred less harmful boasting.

"They cross lanes in seconds taking the innocent with them when they crash. Few who can afford high-speed cars believe in God, let alone in Hermes Trismegistos, the god of crossroads. On impact the twisting knives of sharp, broken metal enter live flesh. The warm tender cocoon of life that enwrapped the rich music of feeling and reason bleeds out with astounding quickness.

"I was always opposed," Elizabeth went on, "to this murderous toll. The long and painful gain we make in our lives so quickly impaled on ragged metal, trickling out whatever we made of ourselves as the lungs rupture and the heart stops. The house of the soul so quickly transformed. I am, in the end, Helen, not ghoulishly inclined, just indignant at this sheer absurdity."

That was the moment they realized the sirens were not coming up the *Autobahn* but from dead ahead, the flashes of red like alien searchlights blinking through the stockades of dark oak trunks which were uncomfortably close on both sides of the road.

The white and green projectile of the German police car came with a snarl, whooping and pouncing as if leaping out from the jungle.

INSPECTOR HORATIO QUEBERON was not at the wheel. He abhorred the speed his police drivers gloried in. His stomach was not pleased either. He had enjoyed a prolonged lunch with the mayor with a perfectly reasonable glass of fine German wine and a steak of Black Angus beef cooked to his liking. Then he had settled to organizing his papers holding a mug of strong coffee. He felt satisfied and moderately pleased with his life. He was not a man of extremes.

Then the call came through. He grabbed his Barbour jacket on the way out. Some fool had fallen into the lake at Woerlitz and they had fished out a body.

The police car gained speed as it came out of the village of Waldersee on the smaller winding road to Woerlitz. Ahead, as Inspector Queberon well knew, were the twists and turns this country road took as it skimmed past the water meadows of the River Elbe.

The tarmac poured like dark snakeskin through the old oak trees. The bigger road was to the south of Waldersee connecting to the *Autobahn*. This minor road they were on was the old connection through the villages. On all sides it was thick with oaks standing close to the road, splendid in the thick grasses. They were grouped in dense packs and crowded by the road. He saw their black trunks ahead. His body tensed as the car dived at speed into the serpentine twists. He had fastened his seatbelt despite his too copious lunch.

The entangled cars were graceful in their dance of death. Like powerful circus lions they embraced and clawed, hissing and scratching. They reared and spun, lacerating each other, shoulder to flank. And peacefully they came to lie side by side, having circled and slid, and come to a halt just short of the stanchion legs of huge oaks.

"There is a God. She was watching over us," said Elizabeth, breathing out.

Her body had sprawled forward awkwardly, yet was held tight and upright by her seatbelt. Helen was out cold, staring ahead, her hands still clutching the steering wheel. Someone was going to have to prise her loose. Her heavy hair had come unbound, falling like water over her forehead and shoulders.

A heavy set but athletic man in a checked shirt appeared suddenly, knocking on their car window, gesturing to Elizabeth. Mercifully, he was able to open the door.

. . .

STILL GRIPPING the steering wheel Helen rested there, slumped forwards. She was in shock. She had come to, but was sliding in and out of consciousness. The ambulance crew that had been alerted for the supposed drowning had caught up and the medics began to prise Helen out, her body heavy and floppy like a department store's manikin.

Elizabeth sat at the side of the road, dazed but lucid. Her black hair had kept its neatness, cropped close like Athena's helmet; she who was beloved of the merciful gods and a spinster like Elizabeth.

The man in the checked shirt and dark green corduroys had managed to open the car door; eased her out. His hand had been shockingly warm as lights and crashing sounds swirled like shooting stars through her blocked senses.

The man who loomed gloomily at her side said he was a policeman, an inspector with the Dessau Police. His grip had been strong, pulling her out and away from the car.

Helen and she had been talking, she thought, about books in their hands, libraries in their heads. Was this Orpheus leading the dead out of the black and red flames of the underworld? But this is not poetry, thought Elizabeth, this is a car crash. I have just survived it. As I survived once before.

"Nothing broken," the paramedic had eventually said,

after pinching and poking her expertly in all the right places. "Can we take your name and place of residence?" another had queried. "She seems quite alert," the one said to the other.

Then the inspector's voice overrode their comments. He said to her, "It was the police driver that took the brunt, broken bones and a concussion. We miraculously escaped an inferno of blazing petrol. The gods were kind; neither car met an oak head on. Instead, we tangoed."

He turned to the ambulance crew and said: "She's foreign, has a British passport and is staying in the cottage called the Eyserbeck House in the Luisium. I found some papers in her handbag. All roads lead to Rome! We were called out to investigate a body in the Woerlitz lake, as you know. Seems the so-called garden kingdom is no paradise. Culture can have its ruthless dark underbelly of death." His powerful frame kicked into stark profile in the glare of ambulance lights.

"How many cars are here now? Get the trade to take the wrecks to a garage, and if she doesn't want a doctor, get another police car to take her to Waldersee and the Luisium."

RETURN

The police driver manoeuvred the vehicle through the barrage of extra cars and the blockade set up on the road and drove very slowly away.

She had been in Dessau for only a few days and already her life wasn't predictable.

She breathed hard. She expelled her breath slowly. She was now in the middle of events that sucked her in. No longer just visiting.

Implosions of violence had been rare in a life devoted to historical research of times past. This was no longer the case. Developments meant she would be investigated.

She noticed the village houses along the main road in

Waldersee, passing as if she were filming a bland post-war drama.

This was the place where she wanted to highlight friendship among women in her lecture. It would now be more than that. She came as a foreigner, yet the present demanded she share the woman she was—historical and real in the here and now.

The police car turned into the parking lot that on its north and west sides was blocked by the big dyke. It had been erected since the last floods because this dell—but not the hill the Luisium stood atop—was inundated regularly. Here too, the Mulde River wound its way to add its waters to those of its bigger cousin the Elbe. There was an inscrutable boundary here, a spiritual border-crossing.

The stark illumination of the streetlamps ceased and the mellow contours of old trees and pathways began. The Luisium was built in gentle terrain, filled with allusions to myths and sacred geometry.

The driver brought the car back to the rutted track on top of the dyke, wanting to follow its windings into the park to the Eyserbeck House. Elizabeth stopped him.

With an effusion of gratefulness, assurances about her ability to cope and a firmness of voice that betokened the desire to be left alone, she got out.

The cold night air on her felt a relief. The near blackness would hide her shakiness, her sudden infirmity.

She stood up very straight, watching the red tail-lights of the police car vanish. She was alone at last, where old pine trees and hemlock wove patches of sombre darkness. The nodding, whispering branches of sweet chestnut gave the air softness. The summer grasses carried sweet smells and assuaged her bruised mind. The night air was balsam. As she stood on the earthen mound of the dyke she saw the faint, pale whiteness of the pebbled paths that would take her to her present lodgings, the former gardener's cottage Eyserbeck House.

She walked in by the granite boulder marking the beginnings of the park. Everything before her was reduced to pure shape. Night had no colour and few clear distinctions. She must gather her senses. She must grip the present and speak out about Louise and Henriette. It might convince the many shuttered houses to open to future happiness.

To her recovering senses it was a relief, the flooding back of her ability to perceive. Now, to her body and mind she reverted to the oblivion as one who is no different from the nature around her. The awakening of her night senses let her read more subtle truths with their welcome distortions of the near and far, challenging the mind to add imagined shades. Imagined but real insight.

Elizabeth did not mind staring death in the face. The

car crash had terrorized her. But it had also loosened something primeval, a flow into consciousness of why she might be here. Friendship was more than precious. People cared whether one were dead or still living.

She was getting involved with the dead, with ghosts and their legacies and how the living treated them. This was, she acknowledged suddenly to herself, the secret double-flooring of her research.

Those floodlit stadiums of factual assertions were but the wrestling matches of professorial power. Elizabeth had always wanted to go deeper. She wanted to find the lives of women in the dark, the neglect and obscurity imposed on them by being in hidden places. Should she die, it was not for her passing that she would grieve but for the work left undone.

She stopped walking. She knew she was only a shadow in this unlit landscape, this veiling cocoon of the unknown. But she would sing aloud, the voice within her would sing out.

Close to her she saw the black density of fir trees and the finer illumination of open lawn like criss-crossing fields of possibility, some light and rational, some obscured and full of questions. On this field thick with energies were the whispering shrubberies and beyond that, in the far distance, the surreal glow of Louise von Anhalt-Dessau's house, the Luisium. Spotlights were trained on its cubic form, lifting it out from the dark in pale moon gold, an emblem, a fourfold tower, a four-square house. A beacon of light.

There were ghosts within, of that Elizabeth was certain. The house was a watch-tower, a listening post in which womanly figures trod the oaken stairway soundlessly. This was why she had come, why she had entertained her own fledgling quest, not knowing where it would take her or how it would change her.

She heard the tawny owls that lived in the high trees of the park, their flight combing the wider landscape in its long sweep to the Elbe. "Who?" she thought she heard them call. "Who?"

She was but a shadow herself. The only illumination in this darkness was the enigmatic cube that sat imperturbable beyond the end of the path to the cottage. There on its mound the fabled cubic temple rose with the moon hanging over it, sharing its pale light while the night remained full of subtle mystery.

RECOVERY

How spick and span this is, thought Helen, waiting for her mother to come and take her home from the hospital. She was in a single room ready to be discharged. The white shimmering curtains hid the sunshine. But the shiny floor still glowed with cleanliness even in the low light. The bed sheets were tucked in tightly. Even the pictures hung straight.

The one she was looking at had diagonals and intersecting planes of colour. It was a Lyonel Feininger print of cathedral towers spearing pale rectangles of sky. Helen shook herself. She must be recovering well as only the idle looked intensely at artwork in hospital buildings. The nurses had no time and the seriously ill were too worried about their fate.

The abstract Feininger's interlocking planes made her giddy, just as her dream had. It had that same quality of slipping and tipping down unfathomable space. Unstoppable motion. Bottomless pit. Then the image had changed to sand running through an hourglass. And it had turned. Then there had been black space again.

Only natural that I dream like this, Helen thought.

But she then remembered an edge glittering just as she reached out to turn the hourglass. This edge shimmered and sparkled at her. It hurt her eyes, spun in her head. She was fainting, in the grip of shadows. This reveals the black figure, she thought, the one I thought I saw surfacing in the lake in Woerlitz, then drowning. She strained her memory.

She couldn't define what she saw. "Lifting a thousand lids, how will you open the six walls of the void?" The line haunted her.

The sound of brisk footsteps coming down the linoleum-floored hallway paused her thinking. They hammered the dream world back into plain-as-day. Only one woman walked with such clipped authority.

Her mother was thin, tall and with short greying hair. She was a retired doctor and not much in the way of man or beast could ever stop her.

"Hello, Mother," said Helen. "Lucky the driver knew how to swerve. All the damage was done by the cars side-swiping each other. I seem to be all right."

Her mother's face was pale and angular. Across it flicked a rueful smile, bright with tasteful lipstick. Her upbeat mood sparkled in her deep blue eyes. Dr Agatha Brecht had completed her medical studies when women were not yet encouraged to become doctors. She possessed an exemplary restrained femininity.

"I think you should come home with me. Give you a chance to catch your breath. No place like home, you know."

"Did you bring some fresh clothes?" asked Helen. "I remember grit and flaky metal all over me. Some blood, too—superficial, of course." This remark she added knowing there would be no false sympathy. She sighed. She would never be able to live up to her mother's heroic view of life. If you survive, don't complain. There are worse things.

"Inspector Queberon is always everywhere and nowhere, as the saying goes. Like the Scarlet Pimpernel, hard to pin down and with virtues like candle smoke. Opaque. I rang his office," her mother said in clipped tones. "It seems your companion was a woman professor from Scotland. Is there such a thing?"

"I met her walking," replied Helen. "In fact, I met her as she fell down the steps of the Temple of Venus, missing that lower step where the sunlight obscures the descent. You remember the pathway down the steps below the temple proper where all visitors have to climb down below and are led into the dark in order for them to appreciate the descent to Hades? She tripped right there. I was coming up into the light and caught her, steadied her. We landed in the big stone Druid's seat facing the actual cave-like chamber below the Venus Medici. There used to be admonishments scrolled on the walls, the light coming in through openings in the stones. These are now illegible. For her it should have read: 'It's not the size of the dog in the fight, it's the size of the fight in the dog.' Her name is Elizabeth Hammerstein. I'm sorry about your Volvo. Did you bring some fresh clothes?"

AS THE CROW FLIES

The crow was black as night and now raised its wing to preen itself. Then, shaking her plumage, she looked to the east. There the long lazy curves of the Mulde edged towards Dessau and left it behind; the eastern riverbanks were unregulated and ragged with dense vegetation. The old overflows of the river were winding through willows and mown meadows. Once this area had been the menagerie where the silver-feathered pheasants imported from England had strutted.

Northeast of the crow's high perch, Dessau eased again into lush water meadows. These were punctuated by the free-standing old oaks growing in solitary splendour near the dykes that wound towards Waldersee and the Luisium.

When the crow finally flew off she went south, her wings beating in the slow rhythms of her tribe. She passed the two water-towers of the city, the one a sorry wreck, the other recently rebuilt in smart post-modern design. It housed the main lecture room for the regional archive. The tower's side was edged in seven storeys of new glass and steel, the other side kept its ornate Victorian brickwork intact.

The enormous cauldron of iron that had once held the city's water supply had been opened and augmented inside by fine arches and even finer pilasters and medieval windows, as if dryness had shape-shifted water storage to keeping innumerable documents. In the tower, next to the remains of the black iron cauldron, were the new modern seats and a lectern for talks and conferences. The rest of the archive curved behind the water-tower's brick frontage, housing archival offices and the reading room.

The archive's modern look was a part of the regeneration strategy in the brief time money flowed east following German reunification. The archive specialised in the history of the region and contained the papers from the House of Anhalt-Dessau.

Its administrative head was Eva Delamotte. She was at present sitting elsewhere, directly opposite to the black crow's flight path, in the Junker Bar of the Hotel Fuerst Leopold. Before her was a shot of Islay whisky, the peaty Laphroaigh, and a small dish of roasted nuts. She was leaning into the lush cushioned sofa to the left of the deserted bar, the water of a fountain lending its calming splash to this post-modern hotel lobby. Above her in the higher reaches of its elevated, copious roof flew a model of the JU 52-3m, Dessau's most famous aircraft "Tante Ju", designed by Hugo Junkers.

It had been one of the first aircraft made completely of metal parts. Now it flew over sofas and the fronds of deep green palms, the whisky and Eva.

The archive closed at 4pm and she wanted peace and a rest. Dessau had the great attraction of not being Berlin, so that this watering-hole, in the late afternoon, was practically deserted. Her mind let go of the concerns of the day. She stretched her long legs and lifted the glass, holding it out along the back of the beige sofa. Her gaze travelled from the reception desk past the revolving door to the front of the hotel where the green treetops of the park opposite shone through and on towards the left to the dining room, now set for guests with brilliant white tablecloths and silver cutlery. The pinpricks of the halogen lighting had always intrigued her, as this was clean 1960s style unspoilt by remodelling. The tiny lights were bright, reassuring, rational even.

Like good weather neither silence, nor peace nor the

slight inebriation she was just noticing were ever going
to last.

The movement of the glass revolving door caught
her eye. It flashed like a warning sign and spilled several
people into the Fuerst Leopold Hotel. Unfortunately,
she recognized some of them.

The man who rushed in first was the head of the
Preservation Society of Dessau-Woerlitz. His white hair
looked as if Eric Gill himself had chiselled it. His nose,
Eva decided again, was definitely that of a whippet.

For some reason he preferred tweed jackets with
patches on the arm and pin-striped shirts to the more
relaxed German style of menswear. He wore his oblig-
atory tie, blood-red with blue dots. Eva slid down and
picked up the local newspaper, the *Mitteldeutsche Zeitung.*
She held it up high, covering her face, hoping to dodge
any greeting.

But Direktor Edwyn Eszett turned his steps rapidly
towards the dining room. He was obviously having a
meeting. The hotel waiters were already sliding towards
him. In tow he had what seemed like young management types. Certainly they were not from here, thought
Eva.

And then Babylonia von Moritzburg burst through
the revolving door.

Everything Babylonia did was done with a bang.
Even the glass door sucked in an extra whistling groan;

her blonde beauty was usually the centre of attention. Whatever she undertook she would be certain to bull-doze her way through. Today she wore sunglasses and a man's shirt with well-cut trousers. She didn't glance about her. And she carried a fat briefcase.

Eva sunk very low into the sofa behind the news-paper but her curiosity was aroused. This was definitely a meeting out of hours and one with hefty players. If you did not want to be convivial or draw attention to yourself, this was the time and the place.

In the dining room she saw the young managers gesticulate and spread papers on the one table not yet set with napkins and floral decorations.

ARCHIVES ARE like the great pyramids, thought Eva the next morning. Buried in the deposits of papers, hand-written or printed, are puzzles and secrets. As the dead depart they slough the skins of their life and give them for safe-keeping to an archive. As these are maintained by the public purse, anyone can read what is in them. But this is not as simple as it sounds. Not everything is minutely catalogued.

Also, the cities on the Elbe were subjected to late spring bombing raids just before the Second World War ended. The bombing of 1945 and the occupation by Soviet troops meant chaos and hardship. The archival holdings in Dessau were hidden in mine shafts and bunkers, but parts were pillaged and taken to foreign countries. After the war some papers trickled back but only piecemeal.

Just like people, these papers were prisoners of war, wounded and badly healed, losing an eye or a hand, eventually limping home.

Eva knew well enough that her grasp of the archival records came through her readers' requests. She had not been working with the deposits as long as some of her predecessors. The *Findbuecher*, the index to the various deposits with their short descriptions of content, were surprisingly uninformative. They only recorded generically, that is, names of correspondents, dates and general topics, such as "papers relating to legacies."

If the reader talked about his or her project she was sometimes able to make suggestions for further research, but she rarely had enough spare time to look at bundles of archival material herself and note what was in them. The general public held the delusional view that an archivist could put her finger on any subject at any time. Some correspondences had not been read since they found their way onto these shelves.

One of her current readers had put it very perceptively by remarking that although the ink no longer faded in the dark treasuries of the archive, the emotions that drove the writing did. Conflict and love, politics and repression, the goose-quill slant in loops and points —completely unlike today's form of writing—held the secrets of men and women whose decisions had consequences into the present. This applied especially to land and legacies.

Her reflections led Eva to muse on Babylonia von Moritzburg and her meeting all those young managers and Edwyn Eszett in the hotel. Babylonia was an extraordinary woman. Not an intellectual by any measure, but effective. Sly, even; certainly grasping. What were her connections with these men? What was she up to?

"O my paws and whiskers," remarked Eva. She had done a lot of reading in British mystery novels. Professor Gervase Fen was her ultimate hero. Laidback, but prone to tempers. "Like myself, really," she reflected. "He knows a lot—anyway, he deduces a lot! Like Fen I trust my instincts. Or run into the wrong people at the right time."

Just then, a car door slammed. Eva looked up from the reception desk past the double doors to the parking spaces. The emaciated form of Dr. Wilhelm Paternoster wavered in the heat. He was thin like a wisp of smoke.

Perhaps sulphur, thought Eva. Here comes the servant of Beelzebub himself. Here is a man who, no matter how he slides forward, can never be whipped into any shape or substance.

"Good morning Dr. Paternoster," she said.

"Oh, good morning Dr. Delamotte," said Paternoster.

"Nice day. Not much rain," said Eva.

"Not much prospect of rain," said Paternoster.

He stood. She handed him his cardboard tray of documents with his name on them. His damp hands circled them, drew them to him. His earring shone in the neon lighting.

Paternoster wasn't telling anyone of his engagement by Babylonia von Moritzburg. And now he was more than triumphant in his innermost being because he had found the necessary fundamentals of Henriette's will. He was sure that Babylonia von Motizburg would inherit the property she was looking for. He had found proof. She could dominate the landscape garden with her new hotel.

But first he would extract his dues. He would become manager. He would finally tell Eszett where to get off.

And the doors to the reading room closed behind him. No-one around here would be any the wiser.

"PERHAPS I MIGHT REVISE my opinion of Babylonia," thought Dr. Delamotte, "if pigs had wings.

"Anyway, the woman has dominant attributes—like blonde, curly hair and marvellous tight clothes—the

mascara blinking above oh so innocent eyes. She might
—who knows—have burst into the archive, plied
everyone with questions while her heavy breasts were
leaning on the reception desk. Why am I letting my prej-
udice show? There's never any shying away from Babylonia in subtle evasion," she moaned. "And how and why
do Paternoster and my beloved Babylonia connect in my
mind?"

Babylonia had never graced the doors of an archive.
But that did not mean she had no means of gaining any
information she wanted. She was wont to research by
proxy. In small towns the powerful used their position
and would send in their assistants. After all, as the crow
flies is only an aerial view of how a city looks. Its actual
streets harbour a multitude of sins. Babylonia could
easily muster helpers for any computer database. She
was able to gain devotees to dig out for her any map of
pathways and desires.

THE SCREEN FLICKED on its restful blues and the well-
known icons. The archivist called up the identification
numbers of recent materials consulted by readers.

All the users called up particular subject areas. Elizabeth Hammerstein's archival interests were perfectly
consistent. "Hammerstein is pursuing what she explains
as research into the narratives of history, the connection

between personal 'life-writing' in letters and other documents and how the contracted or designed landscape became an extension or 'dream landscape' either complementary to or as a vista of changing social aims." Eva pondered as she spoke the words Elizabeth had written down. "Put in a nutshell, she is reading the diaries of Louise von Anhalt-Dessau and taking these as a cue to explore other writings," she concluded.

Slowly Eva reviewed the other readers, and slowly she found that Hammerstein was being shadowed. The calling up of documents was far too similar. Paternoster must be finding what he was looking for by trailing Elizabeth Hammerstein, and she was none the wiser. But what could he be looking for?

INNER SANCTUM

Both the archivist and the inspector had suspicions they were pursuing. And they fastened on these, hoping to be served with tangible evidence. But it was like building a case on footprints in the rain. Eva wondered about the meeting she had observed between the haughty Eszett and the enticing Babylonia with her sombre black briefcase.

Inspector Queberon told himself, "slogging is what I always do at the beginning. Fishing in the dark. Going hungry when I see chicken bones too bare for anything but soup. Hmmm.

"Eszett is elusive and damning when he encounters policemen—I shall interview him. And be at my severe best. I can only hope he gives me some clue to how he's involved. The drug trade is always a question mark."

. . .

Herr Direktor Edwyn Eszett put his glasses on top of his head. It had been a bitch of a day again. Sometimes he felt as if all and sundry wanted him on death row. It came with the job, he reflected. But he liked the fact that he wasn't bereft of the kowtowing that he felt was his due.

He was tall. Willowy, even, and blue-eyed. He hunted with the best of them, all that was left of them, the old aristocracy. These people had charm, their opinions decisive, robust and dismissive.

The best parts of the old Anhalt-Dessau estates were under his management. So what if women felt dismissed by his talking down his nose, like Eva Delamotte and Elizabeth Hammerstein, twisting the long line of his mouth into unsmiling disapproval of these female subordinates. Display a bad temper and everyone, he thought, would tip-toe or think twice about asking him anything.

That goose of a woman, he repeated to himself, that Elizabeth Hammerstein who had once called him a vainglorious rooster, was back in Dessau. An academic who insisted there was such a thing as women's history. He groaned now because he kept himself in check. He had flipped on his deprecatory smile and said he didn't need to be told about history! Frankly, it bored him to tears. He didn't even do crocodile tears. Crocodiles of his creed did not bother with snapping at gnats.

And yet there were deadly enemies among those taking what was labelled 'women's studies'. They wanted to upset his cherished interpretation of the Prince. For it was he, and the Prince alone, who made Dessau-Woerlitz into the kingdom it was today.

Babylonia von Moritzburg was another matter altogether. Nothing wrong with her. She was the kind of woman he liked. She was part of the local gentry. Her marriages past and present gave her vital links to the nobility. And she had that certain something, the promise of sadism, of excitement.

Her hips had that liquidity only the best-sprung of expensive car undercarriages manifested—not that he could afford that kind of car—but he always fancied a fast careen down the *Autobahn.* A Mercedes Coupé was not really a bad car and his driving in the *Dienstwagen* was a pain. The whole German power-car industry achieved nought to whatever in seconds and tail-gating was a sport played against the weak. Let them eat exhaust.

The delicious Babylonia would be here to ask him about something in minutes. Her crisp white shirts were buttoned below the permissible. Her skin was tanned. Her mind was never cluttered with book learning. Her only fault was sensible shoes. He did like heels.

His desk was at the far end of what was once the drawing room of the country house in Kuhnau. This had the intended effect of making anyone wishing to see him pace the length of the room. He could uncoil at leisure and slowly relinquish his expensive fountain pen, cap it nicely, push his mock-turtle reading-glasses up like a movie star. He always squinted as if he hadn't a clue as to why his important work had to be disrupted. He was in charge of heritage, money, the future of the arts.

He heard his secretary knock. She was instructed to knock loudly, then to pause significantly and open the door. Direktor Eszett straightened his tie, lifted a hand to raise his glasses and settled them on his head. He wondered whether Babylonia would stay for lunch.

"Inspector Horatio Queberon," announced his secretary.

The door banged open and in strode the ubiquitous Inspector Queberon. He was never one for shuffling along carpets. His polished shoes covered the distance with naval brevity. He had been with the Navy and was adeptly multilingual as well as multi-cultural. Even the casual jacket he wore sat nicely. He left Eszett standing and lowered himself onto one of the conference chairs at the table some distance from the desk.

Queberon had come on the suspicion he might task the Direktor with some incriminating admission, but since he only had evidence from Hans Homburg's abandoned gondola, this was spurious and Eszett would say it had nothing to do with him. Nonetheless, it was his duty.

He stared somewhat disparagingly at the chintz curtains that were not quite precise in their descent from brass rails. They had an odd green lining.

"Direktor Eszett, how pleasant to find you here and in need of company. As your time is always valuable I will not presume to stay long."

He took out a pocket watch on a golden chain. It was one of Queberon's vanities.

He had always liked the White Rabbit who was recognizable and in a hurry. He had read that book as a child. Come to think of it, it had been read to him by his mother to improve his English. But this was side tracking. He must try to corner Eszett. Straight on.

"I have recovered a body from the lake at Woerlitz. The face has been disfigured and no identification on the body has been found. We have impounded the gondola from which he seemed to have fallen into the water and there is tape all around the shore of the lake near the Nymphaeum. We have temporarily blocked the roads. Height of the tourist season, I know." He paused, watching for any discomfort.

"The dead body is that of a young man, quite fashionable. He wore the sailor's striped top and a black cap.

Drugs were stashed in the gondola's seat. This particular gondola had been loosened from the tourists' collective and taken to the Wolf Canal, the one circling the Gothic House, the preferred residence of the Prince," Inspector Queberon said.

He waited in silence, then continued. "The boy was not from here. He was a playboy, a muscular star of some nightclub. His pockets had keys but no address. One of the drug packets, however, was billed to what could be plausibly made out as one Direktor Eszett."

There was nothing but a slight tensing of the body in a mostly immobile figure. In the greying hair, the blind mock-turtle glasses caught the blank light from the windows.

A moment later, Eszett spun away. "I'm happy you're dealing with this unfortunate interlude in the park. I'll have to adjust the plans, however. I'll give orders to oarsmen to not bring tourists to this evening's concert."

There was to be an evening of baroque music floating out over the water to the tourist-filled gondolas. A select few were paying top prices for the privilege of late evening exclusivity. That income would be gone. Ruined.

Inspector Queberon ran his eyes down the lean figure standing not a few yards from him. A strange combination, this man, he thought. Eszett had the look of a very elegant hound with his nose to the wind. A necessity for the man in charge, perhaps. His work was chatting people up, convincing politicians. A short-cut to influence that went beyond local importance, Inspector Queberon supposed. He gazed more deeply at this man he had only seen once or twice. Even in summer his suits were dark, of that murky tweed brown only the English style got away with, including those ridiculous mock-leather elbow patches.

The man was obviously in a bad mood and Queberon was about to leave him with it intact. He had not gotten much information, or for that matter, much cooperation from him. But the tight-lipped Eszett was never sociable, never friendly.

A closed mouth spreads no rumours. This was one of Queberon's favourite sayings. He had pinned it up over his desk. His own morality was quaint and rooted in the long tradition of the slow boat to heaven. Friends mattered. Sailors had patience if nothing else. Wait and see was never a wrong signpost. And plunge in to save lives.

EDDIES of expensive perfume preceded her as she shipped into the port of Eszett's inner sanctum. "Baby-lonia!" he murmured, "so good to see you." He bent over her right hand and kissed it in the best aristocratic style of a pretend kiss just above her slack wrist. He held her hand a second too long.

She did not withdraw and he knew that there would be some bargaining in the offing.

"I'll sit down if I may," she said, and crossed her long legs and lifted her blue-grey eyes to meet his. The look was expectant rather than flirtatious. He sat down at the conference table, at an angle, so that he could be close and yet business-like. "I won't take coffee," she pre-empted him.

"I have a very special request," she began. "I want to establish a claim to some papers perhaps given to the regional archive by mistake. As you know, there was chaos after Hitler's defeat and as the new government came in. As the archival deposits were taken from their temporary safe-houses in caves or such like—I'm no historian—or trickled back from our friends the Russians, family records may have mingled with the boxes going back to the *Landesarchiv*. It may very well concern you, just as myself."

She paused for emphasis; threw him a sidelong glance.

"As you know, the Anhalt-Dessau lineage is tangled by the so-called marriage *linker hand*, sanctioned alliances with official mistresses, later usually raised into the aristocracy, offspring which are also quasi legit-imate, at least through the last will and testament of their fathers, who, if they have a streak of weakness, provide well for them."

"As you know," and she looked up again with her candid blue-grey eyes, "men had few inhibitions and the power to cause much mayhem, with most social and financial dispositions at their beck and call, so there are Counts with estate names, like Waldersee, and some endearing ones like Berenhorst, and even others, less well documented, like the offspring of the Prince of Anhalt-Dessau's brother Albert.

"This younger son of the reigning Leopold III Friedrich Franz owned separate lands and was divorced from his wife Henriette. There are complications and there might be a last will and testament of extraordinary interest.

"And as I am free after separating from the Duke of Moritzburg and come from a long line of aristocratic alliances *linker hand*, this is of some consequence for you, am I right? I think I have rights to land right next to the landscape garden. If I were to build a hotel there, it would augment your tourist intake."

"Have we not usually seen eye to eye, *mon ami?*" replied Eszett.

The light dimmed in the generously proportioned former drawing room of the Palais of Kuhnau, as one of the frequent summer showers drummed against the long windows, sliding silver jewels of no value but exquisite provenance, down the length of glass.

"I am so glad you could you spare the exquisite Dr. Paternoster for some sleuthing," said the exquisite Babylonia. "He's reading up anyway on material for your next exhibition. So this, my little request, would be perfectly innocuous. I'm sure he will find all the paperwork I require."

The hunting and betting man in Eszett bubbled up like champagne, causing him to feel tipsy. He saw himself climb into that fast car, a stunning Babylonia placing her exquisite aristocratic limbs in the passenger seat beside him.

"Lunch?" he asked.

"Not just now," she said.

NEVER THE TWAIN SHALL MEET

Helen threw the covers straight off the bed. Being bedridden had always sent her into rebellious fits. She felt like the bird in Joseph Wright of Derby's picture being suffocated slowly in the vacuum pump experiment. The wings went limp and the head would droop.

She hated this picture in which the bird was sacrificed to science, the painter using the light to show the rapt attention of the boy and the sentimental hiccups of the girl watching. She kicked at the bedclothes, tumbling them to the floor, then listened to see if her mother was in the house. Silence reigned in the comfortable, well-lit rooms looking out on the old trees and the groomed lawn.

It was a good day to make a dash for freedom. She could sneak out to a bigger city, maybe Halle, three-quarters of an hour away on the train. Take a coffee in the *Kleine Ulrichstrasse* and shop for clothes. Anything but books. She wasn't dead yet. She looked at her green eyes and her fly-away dark hair in the mirror as she brushed her teeth. Lying in bed made her feel her teeth went soggy. The chemical white foam of toothpaste gave her mirror image whiskers. She might be the Cheshire cat she thought, then grinned widely, gargled and spat water into the sink.

She had a cat nature, a tomcat, not a kitten. Maybe a puma; these were silent and pounced suddenly and effectively. They were very independent. She pulled on slacks, shirt and a windbreaker, slung her handbag over her shoulder and took her bicycle lock. Her note was brief: "Gone to Halle. Might be back late. Helen."

Being in the fresh air restored her spirits. The wind was plaiting itself into the treetops. The back road in the village took her past the stork's nest on the roof of a disused barn. There these exotic sentinels in their black and white livery and extraordinary red legs reminded her of all the possible migrations that might be undertaken in life. She waved to the storks in exuberance as she passed below and headed for the small railroad bridge over the Mulde that carried the very infrequent tourist train to Woerlitz.

She always thought it was painted a champagne green because its arches seemed to cha-cha with the river while the young oaks in the water meadows only did a foxtrot. The grasses waved and bent. It was all a run on the wild side as this bicycle path to Dessau avoided the asphalted roads. It cut through to the town where cars were banned. On its sides only the mowers went up and down and there the storks ate the frogs.

HELEN SKIDDED on the rough dirt and stones before she bounced onto the asphalt road, ploughed on and hit the old cobbles in the few streets still intact from the nineteenth century. These were the three or four storey buildings with clean and shiny windows. Her bones jostled and her energy flagged, but Dessau seemed too small, too chained to its declining population, for her to ever stay here, she thought. She wanted to roam the world.

Even meeting Elizabeth Hammerstein seemed no more than a bright cloud reflected in a puddle in these mean streets.

The train station finally loomed dead ahead, barely noticeable it was so bland. The Dessau streetcars screeched past it on their glinting silver rails and the bus stop to the right was a long arc of tarmac. Helen wrestled her bike up the stairs of the station. She was taking her bike to Halle as there she could be quicker into the city on two wheels and with no tram tickets to buy.

She was making for the elevator that would take her down to the passage for her platform. Her train was local and she noticed that a fast train was in, probably from Berlin. People would be changing trains.

The problem was, as she knew, getting the bike into the elevator. The design of such things was always left to morons, she was convinced of it. They would give you room just short of what was needed. This was the case here. Only if the bike was wedged hard against the sides and the handlebars and front wheel twisted as if in the process of decapitation would it fit. She shoved and pushed. She punched the button for up.

The car halted with a lurch. She kicked the bike loose, gave it a muscular push as the glass door opened, misjudged it and flew out with the heavy bike dragging her willy-nilly.

The crash was inevitable. She found herself sitting like a dishevelled stork on a nest of luggage. Her bike had speared a young man. Her fall had landed her on a smart silver case, quite big. Her victim was in the process of removing the dirt of Dessau from his shirt and trousers.

She took a deep breath, smiled brighter than any celestial body, stretched out her hand and decided civility was better than argument.

"My name is Helen Brecht and I do apologize."

He could not be German because he seemed shy. His hair was reddish-brown and he was slightly skinny. "Ummm," he said. He seemed even more foreign when he said, once more, "ummm," and then, "I seem to have been in your way."

The event was a bit awkward, as a crowd was milling about them anxious to use the elevator. There were mutterings and glances like bees swarming and about to sting. But no-one helped the accident-prone Helen or her very recent acquaintance. They would have to dust themselves off.

THE FOREIGNER WAS quick to move. He put the bike on its stand out of the way. Then he resolutely took Helen's hand, helped her up, and grabbed his suitcase.

"You probably need a drink."

She stared at him.

"My name is Hugh Knox and I have never been here before, but may I offer you a drink. Coffee or something; *Kuchen?*" he said. "You look like you are severely bruised and need some time to recover."

The dry humour went right over her head. What she did think was that her train had left without her. Her burst of energy was flagging. She felt tremendously tired. He didn't look like he was filled with testosterone and he looked prosperous enough to afford cake for two.

"Ordinarily no, but this time yes," she said.

"You lead the way," he said.

"I propose having coffee and cake in the Tante Ju bar in the Hotel Fuerst Leopold not far from here. Sofas will be good for our bruises, don't you think?"

He grinned. "Despite the tyre of your bike nearly puncturing my stomach, I will attempt to get there."

THE YELP of surprise came in the middle of raising the steaming hot latte macchiato to her lips.

"You're from where?" she asked again.

"From Scotland. From the University of Glasgow where we have an excellent department of architecture. I have come to do some work in the Bauhaus—a bit indecisive on the theme just yet, because I like to be inspired by what I see."

She wondered if he was going to talk her ears off about himself. But he had come to a faltering end.

She took up the conversation.

"You'll see the other Germany. Not the economic miracle side, but a place and its people twisted and turned in the fisted grip of history. The Bauhaus shone bright hope before the Nazis took over. Ideas flooded into Dessau and its architectural stringencies—its burnished cubical abstractions with their glass and bright, white walls— these challenged the heavy curlicue culture of the *Jahrhundertwende.* Remember the bowed caryatids holding up portals and balconies on the big stone houses in the best quarters of the big imperial cities like Berlin. The men inside all smoked cigars." Her voice carried laughter in it.

"A lassie with brains," he joked. But quietly.

He sat upright and looked at her more closely. But she was still in full flight.

"Tourists come here like bumble bees nosing in the native orchid dreams of the Bauhaus, marvelling at this cradle of modern architecture, then fail to look at what we call the rabbit hutches, the assembled architectural equivalent of the plastic-bag born of the idea of the functional and bestowed upon us for social equality's sake by our comrades in the GDR. I grew up here, you know. I see the *voyeurs* do their day trip, pick out the goodies they want to suck and rush back to Berlin. In May 1945, the texture of a well-planned town with an interesting history went down in rubble in the late revenge on Hitler. Then the post-war division of Germany began and in this corner people scrambled to live. No economic miracle."

She turned fierce eyes on him. He suddenly relaxed.

He was fine with women not cowed by anything. She was not going to flirt. In fact, she was going to treat him as an equal.

He looked up at the model of the Tante Ju airplane replica flying overhead. He even liked this afternoon bar with its expensive coffee and huge sofas. He saw lined up on the illuminated glass shelves by the bar all the Scottish whiskies with the Gaelic names gleaming steadily. The demon drink was polished and ready to go. But no one was drinking. A water feature gurgled somewhere in the background. His new acquaintance was right. Here was a forgotten corner of remarkable decency. At least on the surface of it.

It was a clean slate for him. Except for his aunt. His aunt was somewhere here in an archive. The glorious feminist historian Elizabeth Hammerstein, as he knew from her last letter, had come to Dessau to do some research. He was always happy to winkle her out. That would be his next task.

He turned his mind to these practical matters. "Miss Brecht," he said.

"Helen," she said.

"Helen," he said, "may every bicycle be blessed. I don't have one, but I could wheel yours home for you."

"I think I'll chain it to the hotel bicycle rack." But she added, "I don't see why I shouldn't acquaint you with *the whole* of Dessau and its architectural history. We have oodles of it. And I'm a native."

"Graciously offered, graciously accepted!" he said with Scottish courtesy. And she gave him an address in Waldersee.

VISIONS OF THE PAST

Hugh's aunt, who had just very recently become Professor Hammerstein, was immersed in the impossible handwriting of the eighteenth century in the reading room of the *Landesarchiv.* "Few people," she would have said to him, pointing this out starkly, "realize the nerve-wracking toil that goes into publishing a book. Most see the finished book in its unruffled proof-read serenity.

"Eighteenth century handwriting has no grammar or spelling worth the name. That's because the women who wrote letters or diaries weren't taught in school. They weren't aware of conventions of the written language or consistency. Many girls of the upper classes received some tuition, but often erratically." She pursed her lips.

This was certainly true for the diary of Louise von

Anhalt-Dessau. On the other hand, she had been taught astounding things by the likes of Leonhard Euler.

"Louise learnt things at the very tip of mathematical ingenuity. We, today, aren't even pushed to engage top-notch scientists for our knowledge—we have yet to be convinced of engineering and the race to outer space!" sighed Elizabeth.

Euler was one of the foremost mathematicians of his day and knew his science. Louise for ever after, being influenced by him, had a keen interest in scholarship. And she wrote about what she observed.

"But she was never systematically educated. And she hungered after sufficient knowledge all her life long." Elizabeth suspected that for Louise it was more than ornament, more than intellectual sustenance. She consumed knowledge as Euler had intended her to—and she still looked about her. For Louise the firmament of the heavens would widen only by being inscribed by writing and writing and writing. Of her own scratchy pen.

Elizabeth sympathized with those frustrated women of centuries ago. If she seriously pursued searching the truth of the past—her past—she was isolated. Cheery conversations were few and far between. She knew this. She could fathom it. The silence of the archive enforced it. But she would plough on.

Louise von Anhalt-Dessau used a goose-quill pen of

uneven strokes and she plotted tangles of exotically spelled words in tiny almost straight lines. Elizabeth squinted in her frustration. She looked at the lovely blue skies and rolling clouds outside the window and at the ticking clock. The archive shut at four.

Elizabeth was determined. She straightened her slumped back. She read again the passage she had so laboriously transcribed. It concerned the friendship between Louise and Henriette. There were bridges to be crossed here, emotional ones, sentimental ones, bonds of friendship.

"Scholarship is such a lonely business—and who could I talk to, even if I were to find a café?" she murmured. "Dr. Eva Delamotte? She's such a professional, and would never intervene in my conclusions." Yet Elizabeth threw a glance towards reception. She hankered after support, involvement.

In Louise's time friendship seemed real, an emotion treasured, no matter in which gender it found its place. This language of friendship was purpled with rich exclamation, with declarations of effusive affection.

This expressive word-rich dedication in diaries and letters always astounded her, as if to the women, catching their feelings in words made them less ephemeral, less caught in time.

Were there really ghosts which gazed longingly and censoriously through the ages?

Here were moments recollected in the up-slant and down-curve of the goose-feather pen that brought back the daylight of centuries ago.

Elizabeth read to herself words that caught an after-noon on the lake in Woerlitz so long ago. It called to mind the stray gondola Helen and she had witnessed crashing in erratic fashion not so long ago. Elizabeth shook her head to clear it.

The gondola that Louise and her friends took so many years ago had been adrift on mellow azure waters. And not at sunset. The women were speaking in French to keep their words to themselves and beyond the reach of the gondolier. It was hot and sunny with cloud-galleons floating in blue infinities above.

Friederike Brun, a writer and recent friend of Louise, was on her way to Italy, but on a visit to Dessau.

Friederike was the daughter of a pastor from northern Germany and had married one of the richest merchants in Denmark. Her face was round and she was diminutive, clothed in light cotton gauzes that shim-mered. Her heart ached after beauty and she gathered in expression upon expression, a spindle full of words that she wove into her diaries and her poetry.

She worried about Louise and shrouded her in veils of sadness even among the sparkling reeds and summer diamonds of the noontide sunlight on the lake.

Louise's eyes, Friederike wrote, were enormous with

shadowed pain. She was tall and elegant, languorous in her movements, with just that lack of vigorous joy that indicated the weightiness of her sorrow.

Louise had finally conceded the mirage of her ever finding happiness; while her husband the Prince, on the other hand, dallied with his mistress. Louise was contemplating coming with Friederike on her travels south to Italy.

Friederike wrote: "Louise stretched her hands towards me in the gondola and placed a wreath of flowers she had gathered herself from the wild blue-speckled meadows on my lap. She touched my warm hand with her elongated, manicured fingers, trailing them over my skin. Her eyes were expressive of her hope, now, or in the near future, or very, very soon, that the wheels of our carriage might turn on the dry dust of the road south. She seemed, fleetingly, to glimpse joy again. It would be the joy of escape, perhaps the joy of relief, certainly the casting off of her melancholy.

"Louise said to me: I feel the love of poetry in you. I know that in seeing beauty even in its despair, you, like me, would want to exist outside these quickening days despite their sunny gifts and catch everything forever in recollections, in words that will hold us forever together on this lake, on these gentle lapping waves. I want to give you this necklace of opals, a token of esteem."

Louise von Anhalt-Dessau added: "Only once before

have I felt so close to someone. That was Henriette, who married Prince Albert, my husband's brother. She too was unlucky to have been chosen for an arranged union. She wept when she was pregnant. I was her confidante."

Then Friederike recorded her response. She added: "Louise turned her beautiful, strongly-chiselled face with its brown up-combed hair away. She trailed her hand in the water of the lake. It had turned to quicksilver as clouds began to ship closer in a sky hinting at summer storms. I knew little of Henriette except that, having seen her portrait, her smile was like the crescent moon and she seemed ethereal.

"The swaying gondola was turning back. We loved one another, all three. We understood this. This was not, nor could it ever be, physical love; it was deeper than that. Friendship runs deeper than anything physical because it is not a bargain of selfishness, of pleasure gained through the body of another."

Elizabeth read again what Friederike had written about her friend and the inclusion of Henriette; her experience of closeness, of being loved.

"I suppose this is what I am after," she thought to herself, exploring what words do and how they are handed down. "This tender love among women that shines like a summer day even now. This loyalty between these three friends that gives women their distinctive voice even as they look into the future, joyful or afraid, into every changing fate that comes their way."

She wasn't aware of the ghostly nodding of beautiful shawled heads behind curtains at the window. The ghosts liked their words reread and mused over. They were keen to have them taken to the present, looked over and used to good effect. They didn't feel the counting of the years between were of any consequence.

"Mary Wollstonecraft in the British Isles," Elizabeth reflected, "wrote about the rights of women shortly after these effusive words, in 1796, when the French Revolution was in full swing. She was adamant about the rights of women. I know all of this, but I want to know more about Henriette and of the friendship she encouraged— and the others took up.

"But why?" she reflected. "Is it curiosity alone? Or is there something fundamental to be learned from women of the past? A depth of feeling? The richness of feeling without physical entanglement? Friendship that was an alliance that passed even beyond the restrictions of time?"

Elizabeth looked up at the trailing clouds in the window, giant sailing albatrosses to the freshening west wind. "Cloud-catcher. Dream-catcher," she murmured, "that is what I am."

Handing back the cardboard tray with the many folders she had requested, Professor Hammerstein rubbed her tired eyes and smiled. Dr. Eva Delamotte felt overwhelming support. She thought that Elizabeth Hammerstein was putting heart and soul into these researches in an archive so far from her home.

Elizabeth said, "I always feel like a painter setting out to do an historical tableau. First come the innumerable sketches, seeking to position the figures. Did Princess Louise von Anhalt-Dessau write any additional letters to her friend Henriette? These must have been lost. I cannot find them. More's the pity."

"But there are other signs of friendship," replied Eva. "Henriette commissioned a jeweller to remake the golden capsules of the knitting needles she gave to Louise. She wanted Louise to have them as a clasp on her purse. That was Henriette's gift renewed to the maturing Louise. She made sure of continuity.

"I am not sure what else there is in the repository of Louise's private correspondence or her other papers."

Elizabeth countered, "Some would think it local colour. But I think it much more valuable than that. Suddenly, reading about these gifts of Henriette's, and what you said, and what is noted down in Louise's diary, we begin to see any number of connections."

The two of them, archivist and scholar, beamed at the highlighting of friendship and emotional commitment. They liked what they were sharing in the discovery of researching old papers, papers which seemed like new.

Elizabeth went on, "the two women cared deeply for each other. Their birth dates, 1751 for Louise and 1753 for Henriette, make them near contemporaries. Henriette's gift, the changing of golden knitting needles to the gold clasp of the purse, recognises Louise's domestic inclinations, but also, in that first gift, the knitting of wool into patterns, her own joy in creativity.

"Both are ladies of noble birth. Henriette did not give Louise a book, although she easily could have. At the Countess of Rheda's residence, where Henriette lived for a time, she even wrote on philosophy."

Professor Hammerstein continued, looking Dr. Delamotte directly in the eyes, "I think she gave her the knitting needles because she knew that knitting solved puzzles, gave time to engage on a course of action. But I have not a shred of evidence for that, of course!

"What I do know," she added, "is that 'Sentimentality', as historians like to name this kind of reciprocity, ended in true and loyal endearment. These women used their effusive language to manifest their emotion and commitment. The ability to feel strongly comes to light here. Women themselves built very strong bridges. They defined what friendship is. Our ability for independence begins here."

Dr. Delamotte quipped: "Surely a historian's job is to make two plus two equal five!"

Professor Hammerstein laughed: "I am sure the gold casings of knitting needles were indications of status and a rise in GDP. Still, I'm free to pursue female embellishments that seem frivolous to others on the face of it.

"Dr. Delamotte, be sure never to ignore those black on white angels' wings that flutter from the pages—and lift past thoughts into our own present age. The written page often wrings the heart, although we're not allowed to show it!"

And with that Elizabeth waved good-bye, putting on her black raincoat as she flew through the door to catch the tram. Eva remembered that she didn't drive. She either took public transport or rode her bicycle. A remnant of her Oxford days, no doubt. A version of knitting.

LIBRARY BOOKS

The library and not the archive housed the collections, or what remained of them, of the House of Anhalt-Dessau, as Elizabeth well knew. The familial sub-branches such as the family related to the Lippe-Weisenfels, the family of Henriette, left some of their deposits there. The eighteenth-century ones were nicely bound in leather. And Elizabeth liked the feel of this when she was given them by one of the librarians.

The autographs and letters of many of the Prince's counsellors and advisors, on the other hand, were encased in manila folders. As in all special collections no one was really certain about quite what was contained in the boxes and on the shelves. So Elizabeth had her work cut out for her.

She knew that everything was catalogued in every library and archive there is, but she steeled herself as her work progressed because no one exactly knew the contents of each box or book. Again—and this was both the tedious side—and, when revealing secrets, the exciting side of her work—she was happy to dive in. She was of the opinion that the researcher unlocks the content—and the historian puts the content into context.

At present, instead of the archive, Elizabeth engaged in another visit to the Wissentschaftliche Bibliothek. There she hoped to find even more background to the lives of Henriette and Louise.

Elizabeth's motives were radical in nature, but straightforward. Those of Paternoster were not. He had, however, got there before she did. He planned to smuggle Henriette's testament—here and in the archive —out. His burglary—and he relished the fact—was instrumental for Babylonia's inheritance.

Elizabeth walked up to the desk, where Mrs. Emma Specht was holding out to her the key to locker No. 5, where she was to deposit her briefcase and belongings.

Mrs. Specht was tiny as a bird but had the cool eye of the raptor. She knew her vast collection on the shelves and the vagaries of their shelf marks. As the concert pianist plays to effect on the black and white keyboard, she was able to locate what was wanted at a mere hint. The storage spaces were her musical score sheet.

Elizabeth greatly cherished how Emma Specht divined even far-fetched relationships, hidden plans and book affinities. Thus she could suggest a book the researcher had little inkling existed, but that was crucial to the matter in hand. Librarians of Mrs. Specht's calibre were rare. She was a classic to be venerated, and Elizabeth was cheered when she saw her.

"Did the Sachertorte turn out to your satisfaction?" asked Elizabeth, let into the secret of the true heart of Mrs. Specht's interests. Books were only the veneer; she was actually enamoured of the art of the pastry cook.

Emma Specht spoke in the manner of the specialist: "The chocolate glaze, professor, has to be the exact temperature of human blood. It must glide like baby's skin smoothly over the evenly baked, chocolate-saturated cake. And that special lick of apricot jam just under the glaze, at the very top of the cake, well, it's like the synopsis of a book on the dust jacket. Either it's tart enough to awaken the appetite or it becomes the ticket to obesity.

"Cooking's an art, more subtle, most assuredly, than the runny honey poured out to lure the common hoverfly." Mrs. Specht's face widened with a broad smile, the slant eyebrows like double exclamation marks.

Elizabeth chuckled. Her habit of working from

opening to closing in the library had earned her credibility with Mrs. Specht. Gradually she had been let into the secret life of the librarians, all on low pay, all of them women.

Elizabeth had first been asked, tentatively, if she liked baking, an ambiguous question and a puzzle to her in the midst of ordering such tomes as the works of the Dessau poet Friedrich von Matthisson. That had been on her trial visit to Dessau from Berlin. Low-key discussions on how to make meringues rise successfully she astutely recognized as an examination question. They were testing her to see just how eligible she was to be admitted to that select club here in evidence of intelligent but unobtrusive womanliness.

"It depends on the eggs, their freshness," remarked Mrs. Specht.

"And the trick of separating them at room temperature," replied Elizabeth. They had bonded for life.

Emma Specht threw a sidelong glance at the 1950s glass partition that muffled any sounds in the reception area. It would keep their words from anyone in the reading room.

A little frisson of apprehension ran down Elizabeth's spine. She saw a dark masculine form hunched over a pile of books in leather bindings.

She looked more closely as she came back from locker No. 5, exchanging the notebooks cradled in her arms. She stood just outside the glass partition. She was astonished. There in the dusky reaches of the book-laden room, illuminated like some film-noir criminal, with the light beaming upwards from the Fifties swan-necked reading lamps, a shadowy man was bowing, then leaning closer, attentive to scratchy, hand-written testaments before him. This man was gesticulating oddly with white gloves on.

His hair was close shaven and his ears angled out at a devilish tilt. Brow and chin were distorted in the angled electric light, giving the face taut lines of cruelty. Elizabeth recognized the gold and leather bindings of the books from the library of the Princess Louise of Anhalt-Dessau. And she saw the pieces of paper almost hidden below. There were several, and they were in the clear handwriting of Henriette.

The man had close-cropped hair and his ear was pierced on the right lobe with a small golden ring. The white surgical gloves gripped the yellowed, heavy, eighteenth-century works. Then a hand waved like a schoolmaster's, emphatic and relentless, turning the page like a Barbarian conquering civilisation. The front of his polished shoes pushed forward like scimitars, all shiny, where the lamplight pooled on the wooden floor.

"Dr. Wilhelm Paternoster is here," whispered Emma Specht, turning her head away.

BUNNAHABHAIN

Elizabeth was more than surprised to see Hugh coming to visit her in Dessau in the Eyserbeck House near the Luisium.

"I came in a taxi, Auntie. I'm doing work for my thesis on the Bauhaus and Mum said that fits in well as you are now here. So I upped sticks. And, as ever when I come to visit, the unexpected happens. Knowing your addiction to slow modes of slow transport, you'll be pleased to know I was knocked down by a bicycle as soon as I got off the train.

"Only the best women ride bicycles," he added disarmingly.

"You were in an accident already?" replied his Aunt.

"She was quite beautiful, and after her apologies, she helped me find Waldersee and the Luisium. Bicycles leave splendid tracks of black and blue on your solar plexus. And I got a cup of good coffee out of it."

"Stop not making sense, Hugh," said Elizabeth. "I'm glad you got here and were able to find me. I know you're an awful tease, but how do bicycles come into this?"

"She's lovely," sighed Hugh.

"A bicycle?" snorted Elizabeth in disbelief.

"My disastrous first steps into Dessau," said Hugh, "were curtailed by a mad female bicyclist. I was stopped in my tracks, literally, by a beautiful native. Her name is Helen."

"You could go far and fare worse," Elizabeth laughed at him. "As the fates keep muddling human destinies, and I know only one Helen here in town, would that be Helen Brecht?"

After an exchange of incredulity, their conversation swerved back on family matters. And Elizabeth wanted to know more about Hugh's research on the Bauhaus. She proposed he stay for supper.

"We'll toast your arrival after a walk. The sunsets are dramatic from the path on the dam and you can appreciate the Luisium."

"Who is she, Aunt, this women it seems the House is named after? This woman who seems to be causing you and librarians all the trouble?"

He wondered if the trouble was with those who were

dead, ghosts from the past, or with the living, those starchy, unbending academicians with whom Elizabeth always had catfights.

She seemed now to be talking about the dead.

"Dominant. Not to be dismissed. Proud and heartfelt. Louise von Anhalt-Dessau was born in 1751 and lived her 60 years in one of the most progressive principalities of the country, advancing the German Enlightenment. She wrote down what she felt, too, reams of it. She left an extensive set of diaries.

"But that legacy was twisted. Not a decade after her death the biographer of the Prince made her into a hag and a bitter one at that. She was seen as an appendage, hypochondriacally blinded by mysticism. Louise was blamed as the weak and ineffectual woman that drove the Prince into the arms of his young and sprightly mistress."

Elizabeth continued, "The Prince had several illegitimate children. His biographer was a Lutheran orthodox pastor appointed no doubt with the Prince's approval. The churchman made it sound plausible that Louise was cold and frigid. Hence the gardener's daughter as mistress and separate lodgings for the Prince. In the Gothic House."

"Aunt, I love the way you cut to essentials. A whole pack of footnoters will give chase."

"But Hugh," laughed Elizabeth, "it's true! I can always

tell when I hit the truth by the flak I get. I floated this one to the venerable historians of the International Centre for the Study of the Enlightenment and they frowned. Not enough research, they said. And they practically said I was too old for this. Only the radical young held forth on subjects like this.

"They are not partial to old ladies. Especially not ones that speak out and are not of their own making. I don't cite their works. I can't cite their works. They quote the old church hack as if it were gospel truth. I'm blacklisted, by the way. No more invitations to their specialist symposia on the Enlightenment."

"Are your tears real?" asked Hugh. "Or are you going quietly?"

"Hugh! Actually, it's not a joke. I have watched again and again how women are manoeuvred to the edge, their voices petering out. The Germans call it *abseits.* It means you've left the playing field. I'm here pretty much on my own."

Hugh caught the quaver in the voice no one else would have heard. He knew her to be both courageous and vulnerable. The cost of being independent was always there, although it hardly ever showed. He had loved her as a child and he loved her now. He kissed her on the cheek. "I know there's integrity in never bowing to authority. I know your mind. You have no fear in your mind."

"I don't think the Germans here know how innovative this principality of Anhalt-Dessau and its landscape garden was—here on the edge of the Enlightenment! They see it merely as an architectural style that ushered in the great Friedrich Schinckel of Berlin. A new style! My god. I have no end of delight in thinking what they missed by being so pedantic. The glory of this place is that it celebrates British parliamentary Liberty on the very edge of Prussia's drive to military power. You'll hear me out, Hugh, as a romantic Scotsman!

"I'll tell you about an episode with American visitors in Edinburgh," Elizabeth said passionately. "We had all gone to see the Scottish Ballet perform *Romeo and Juliet* just down from the Robert Adam building of the University. It was cold and dark. We were going to walk to Chambers Street where the car was parked. I asked if they had seen the inner court of the Adam building. They hadn't. I took them in.

"We were alone. The spotlights accentuated the tympanums on the temple fronts and the Corinthian pillars caught surreal glints in the scrolls and acanthus leaves from their bright light. The rustications bore up the temples as their proud foundations, just as Adam envisioned it. The rhythms of fan lights and arcs and the abstracted curves of the Baths of Diocletian encircled us.

"The language of men wanting a civil society, the

ideals of the Enlightenment, and freedom of speech, the greatest accomplishment of the British Parliament, wove together in this elegant, mute, testimony. Edinburgh University spoke silently for all republican cities enshrining liberty.

"I turned to my American friends and said to them, here is where it really began, the bringing down of absolutist monarchy. The thread to Benjamin Latrobe and the architecture of Washington, D.C., those exacting balances of power, the fine thoughts of the Declaration of Independence, took flight through the veins of this architecture, the lofty pen of symbolic thought birthing these stones and their enduring message. Darkness enclosed us and left only the spotlights dancing on that sober, Scottish championing of liberty. And no one would know what it meant without it being read in the light of historical knowledge.

"Here at the court of Anhalt-Dessau they used the same language, inspirationally, if not actually, in the homage to liberty. Erdmannsdorff used Palladian architecture, what we call neo-classicism, which Lord Burlington brought to London when he built Chiswick House.

"Our own glorious Scottish architects Robert and James Adam made the style wildly popular and fashionable. They and their patrons were celebrating renewal, the clever adaptation of Roman design and Greek temple architecture, to laud something else: their own ideas of republicanism. Lord Burlington resigned from his position at court to cultivate art and nature as if it were high-brow guerrilla warfare. The Whig progressives did the same. They built the temple-like mansions, seeing themselves as the modern epitome of liberty. The Adam brothers built and designed for these parliamentarians, many of them in opposition, many of them advocates of peace with America, even as the war started in 1775.

"The Luisium was being built just then. Lord Shelburne, or Sir William Petty, Lord Fitzmaurice, as Franz von Anhalt-Dessau got to know him, signed the American peace treaty in 1783. He was an officer in the Seven Years' War, when French troops were engulfing German territory, and British troops fought hard to help the beleaguered Frederick the Great. The Prince of Anhalt-Dessau visited Lord Shelburne in Bowood, his great country house that Adam designed."

They rounded the gates from the Eyserbeck House to the path that led them towards the Luisium.

Hugh saw rising on the small knoll beyond the sweet chestnut trees the soft yellow house with its pyramidal roof whose windows surveyed the countryside.

It was the simplest house he had ever encountered. The proportions were sections of the cube, the two main storeys comprising a perfect one. There was no ornamentation, only the complete surreal composition of glorious plainness, shining in its Aeolian brightness on green canopies and shimmering grasses.

Beside the house Hugh could see the arc of a white bridge, a companion piece of exotic scrollwork, a Chinese intricacy of characters, reflected perfectly in the crescent lake it spanned, so it looked a double bridge, one in the real world and one in the ephemeral whimsy of the water's reflections.

This, thought Hugh, was the world of the mind that perceives and imagines. In our learning we cross the water on this supernatural bridge, minding our feet, seeing the world from the depths we cross.

She was smiling at him and talking. He heard her again.

"There, we will walk the dam and watch the sun setting. The house is on an exact east-west alignment. As the last rays sink westwards they touch the windows and the fires play an eerie orange flame on the blind sheets of glass. I like to think of it as the energy emanating from this house."

"And Louise was happy here?" asked Hugh.

"Probably not, but sufficiently in love with life to wrestle with its demons. I think her house was a second skin, the hull of the boat she pushed out. Place, you know, has apotropaic qualities, it keeps a certain magic in, and this one was the house of the muse. The poetry she revered in life has remained in its good harbour.

"There you can see the white encasing of a small spring she had raised to the powers of Pegasus, the winged horse of poetry. Its attending nymphs feed the winged god and the fountain flows with clear water. Her whole garden is sculpted from water meadows, the overflow of the Mulde River that these dams we are walking on were constructed to contain. And there you see its ancient inhabitants, the white storks."

A mower was cutting the ripe grasses and as they fell two storks on their red legs followed. The frogs and insects dislodged by the blades were speared and eaten. The storks were elegant aliens in white and black dress with long red beaks.

"Folk belief has them bring the babies, as you know, Hugh, so be careful! But sadness too comes with Adebar, as the Germans call him, dropping babies down the chimney. Some hopes ended in false pregnancies, a sorrow common to both Louise and Henriette."

"Are you working on infanticide and doctors again? I thought you had left the medical themes behind?"

"You never leave behind what you know, Hugh. The high jinks of political history are often dependant on the hand of women. Dynasty was after all based on the woman producing the heir. That was fundamental to all the arranged marriages and the settlement of property and inheritance. Titles and estates hinge on it. In Great Britain you had primogeniture, the estates going to the first-born son. Here it wasn't so clear. There had to be much negotiating. Anhalt-Dessau accrued slowly, as the lines died out. Money followed births—or the lack of them."

"Are you onto something, Auntie?"

"Only interested in the mists of time. And how Hecate, the goddess of fate and death, snapped the threads of life."

They were opposite the stud on the western edge of the Luisium. A young colt raced out from the grazing herd. The high grasses were backlit by the setting sun. Its rays caught the flying mane and tail and emblazoned them with light. It looked as if Pegasus himself had leapt into the fine grasses of summer and was galloping exuberantly between heaven and earth.

It seemed to Hugh here was a place exceptional in its dreamy presences. Neglected in the modern sense of commercialised heritage, it possessed that second sight gained by slow motion, by taking one step after another like sleepwalking, and its mood enveloped them both.

Elizabeth was talking again, picking up her own threads of thought that perhaps wove like the late beams of the sun through the foliage. Hugh saw her far-away look.

"I know you wonder why I come to this place. It is a

byway in every sense. But it is in the lost places that unexpected things happen."

They were rounding the southernmost path on the dam, and it opened the long vista towards the Luisium. It was dusk and Hugh saw the black feathery trees frame the plain translucently lit house, in this light cast in shadow in the east and washed with brightness in the west. The sun had almost set. The long sightline through the trees took away common sense and supplanted it with the aureoles of otherness. One could not measure its size or its purpose. It flew into sight like a popinjay of exotic birth alighted on the darkening meadow. The past slept in its blank windows. The ghostly women whose abode it had been had shuttered its inner spaces.

Elizabeth was in shadow, too. Her voice reached Hugh like the flutter of a bird's wing. "Louise and Henriette walked here when they were unhappy. Louise had just been told that the baby she carried was nothing but a ghost, a figment of her longing. The doctor, a stiff bulldog with not a whiff of grace about him, had informed her of her *fausse couche*.

"Louise and Henriette sought relief and comfort in this garden. Walked these paths at sunset with their arms clasped around one another. The beauty made her last pregnancy poignant. They walked here on the path on the dam to look over the meadows, saw the lovely mares swishing their tails in the surreal light and the colts and fillies mad with energy, exuberant in the backlit pastures, the dancing seed-heavy grasses.

"I come here, Hugh, because places have voices. They speak to those who listen."

Elizabeth took his arm. They went slowly back to the Eyserbeck House, strangers here, but deep in the heart warriors whose quests were part of their soul. On the oak table they ate and raised, each, a glass of Bunnahab-hain in the traditional Scottish toast 'to absent friends'.

WITNESS STATEMENT

A curiously hygienic place, thought Inspector Queberon. He surveyed a room that was a cross between the ultra-modern and the homely. The glassed-in steel construction was certainly of recent date. He was in what might be called, with a certain amount of latitude, the coffee room of the archive in Dessau. The light most assuredly benefited the potted plants growing next to the table by which he sat. Their plethora of leaves reflected the sun.

On the other hand, the coffee from the machine was thick and full of chemicals, decidedly unhealthy and produced by a machine that spat and hissed. It disgorged a black liquid that came in shiny plastic cups. He handed one to Elizabeth Hammerstein, who was sitting opposite.

"This is all they have here. The coffee desert stretches all the way to the *Kornhaus* on the Elbe River, that is, all the way across town. The proprietors of that restaurant originally came from Austria. I was lately sitting on the terrace there drinking their *melange.* It had just enough sweet brewed, fresh coffee balanced with less than half again of hot milk. Not *café au lait* and not 'white' coffee as the British would have it. I watched the wide pulse of the Elbe sweep past. Dessau has its moments. The seasonal swifts are catching their insects almost in the clouds, almost as proficient as historians with their facts." He laughed quite pleasantly, but eyed her intently.

"We historians are just second cousins to your own trade," countered Elizabeth. "Birds of a feather, almost. I fly high and pick out little things until, in aerial perspective, the picture clicks. That's the work we do.

"But it would be your kind of swift that have their minds on how and where they roam. Despite the big picture you construct, and even when you go after each insect, you hunt the proof. You cover the most ominous war zones. The judges have to convict, otherwise—the criminal escapes," said Elizabeth.

And she laughed. "Historians and detectives both go after clues, extract plausibility, and then argue their case."

He liked her eyes. They had depth. She seemed always to listen on a deeper plane. "I don't disagree," he said. "Have you recovered from our less formal introduction?"

"Thank you. I am more than ever convinced I like riding bicycles. You see more that way," she added.

"I'm particularly interested in that," he said. "I was called to a death scene in the Woerlitz lake when we had our *pas de deux*. As you may know I went there after seeing that Helen Brecht and you were taken care of by the medics. Now I need to interview witnesses. Actually there aren't any, except you and Miss Brecht."

"You're asking much as if I had seen the Loch Ness monster, I'm afraid," said Elizabeth. "There were ripples and splashes. I saw a gondola in the distance. I put it down to revelry or devilry, really, by some teenage prankster whose intake of spirits produced the wild urge to dunk himself or his mates. Or was this culpable caprice?" Her tone was light.

"Just the facts, ma'am."

Inspector Queberon wanted to know what Elizabeth had seen in as an exact rendition as possible. He was interested in every detail, but he did not know yet where this would lead. He especially wanted an explanation—or better yet, an incrimination—of the pastry cook recently arrived at the Orangerie in the Luisium.

"We were walking back to the large parking lot beyond the Eisenkranz hostelry currently undergoing refurbishment and took the paths by the lake, just beyond the *Englische Sitz*. We were rounding the lake and on its northern shore. I was talking and looked up over the lake. In the far distance (it was nearly dark), there by the trees near the bridge by the canal—the one that goes up to the Venus temple and to the Gothic House—a gondola nudged out. It went broadside. Something splashed. I took little notice as I was deep into explaining something to Helen.

"Yes, I was explaining that the banker Henry Hoare II built Stourhead to link republic ideals with pastoral idylls. Nature in the garden, as he styled it, was a return to a secular belief in the goodness of man. The English Seat reminded him of ideals of liberty and the founding of early Rome governed by the Senate and not yet by emperors. It was replicated with the same ideals in mind."

He was too polite to interrupt.

"The garden here became an emblem of plutocratic responsibility. The young reigning Prince here—he was only 18 when he ascended—dreamed the same, gouging out the lake and the canals to bind together a mythic kingdom; one, actually, that survived against the odds of communism, wars, and rising property values."

An idea struck.

"Around the Eyserbeck House—which I am renting, you know—many people assemble, cooks and clients. They visit the Orangerie restaurant—a lovely place to gather and disperse. The River Mulde is nearby. So are innumerable walks—nothing but trees.

"What if these landscape idylls were used for trafficking? I mean we must perceive what is actually in front of us, a garden with canals—not just the fingerprint on the handle of the gun; if you'll allow me to put it that way.

"I want to tell you why—to me at least—the cooks and certain clients are suspicious."

"Men in white suits with fat bellies?"

She looked at him with a glint in her eye. "Precisely, although I have seen some as thin as spaghetti. They meet where I am staying, sitting at picnic tables by the *Orangerie* opposite the Eyserbeck House. And don't ever tell me cooks are healthy. They smoke cigarettes here in Dessau like chimneys. I suspect the cooks are harbouring secrets, a mafia of sorts. I doubt they are discussing their love lives."

"What has this got to do with my inquiries, my dear professor?"

"Inspector. I saw a flash of bright white disappear in the gently lapping splashes of the gondola death you are investigating. I think it was a bag. It was big enough to catch my attention. Did you retrieve this? Who was it for?"

Queberon was about to ask for more specific detail, but there he had to leave it.

"Ah professor," said a third voice suddenly. The archivist, Dr. Eva Delamotte, descended the short stairs into the visitors' common room, casting an appraising eye on the shiny leaves of the potted plants. "I see, professor, you are solving crime in the company of our illustrious head of police. May I join you?"

Eva Delamotte dropped a coin into the devil's own coffee machine and it hissed and spat. It pissed down the world's worst coffee into a shiny plastic cup.

Inspector Queberon stood up and shook hands as was the custom in Germany. Sitting down again, he surreptitiously poured his coffee into the plant pot nearest him. He hoped the plant would survive.

Eva noticed but overlooked his criminal act. She quite liked the Inspector. He was an easy-going and polite man who didn't push his rank. Anyway, his taste in clothes was just like hers: smart. These days the three-day beard fuzzed the jaws of men far too frequently, reminding her of man's descent from the ape. And they wore things scraped out of the washing machine. The Inspector obviously knew how to dress and was worthy of the two hundred years or more spent learning the use of knife and fork.

Eva cleared her throat. "I am inviting a select few to my midsummer birthday party. I have reserved a gondola out of hours and lots of good food and drink will be on it. Please say you will both come."

ARCHIVAL MATTERS

After he had gone, Eva turned to Elizabeth to say, "I did particularly want to speak to you because of your interest in Henriette. As you know, I trawl through all the literature I can relevant to our archival holdings. In the more obscure journals I found reference to her and even a picture. I'm sure you will be pleased to see this. I felt an intense pleasure when I discovered it. I was particularly taken by her portrait.

"Judging from her short life and her disastrous marriage and her conversion to Pietism, they were called Moravians in Britain, one expects judgemental eyes fierce with conviction—she was a Countess born to a family with impeccable ancestry—but, and this is like a gift handed down to us, she is not at all gloomy.

"Her portrait shows her slim and engaging, nothing doe-eyed about her, nothing flinty, and she has the most brimming, welcoming, happy smile on her face. She seems perfectly in possession of her body and mind and practically steps out of her portrait to meet you."

"It's as if she would like to get to know us," mumbled Elizabeth. More loudly she said, "What a find! I spend weeks and months ferreting out women's biographies. At first I have no more than names and dates. Boring as luggage tags.

"Then some odd insight escapes while reading the papers in the bundles. I was reading in Louise's diary and I realized how violent the emotions felt by these women were. I wondered at the high pitch of all these writings. And then of course one tracks back and looks at deficiencies that cause these needs. You begin to wonder what the qualities were that attracted such fervency—and don't say from the jaded pinnacles of our liberated times that this was suppressed lesbianism or wisely mothball it in the rubric 'sensibility'.

"Jane Austen thought following one's feelings a recipe for disaster. I am beginning to think now that women were truly wise in keeping their feelings out of their arranged marriages. Their common fate, their gendered fate, gave them common ground for at least describing their feeling to one another, however. So they were fortunate when they could at this juncture show their feelings for each other.

"What I am cogitating about in front of you, my learned friend," Elizabeth smiled in her most engaging manner, "is sensibility as strength, and friendship among women as a safety net for exploring difficult emotions.

"Such an insight lets me see how women cope with all sorts of pain on so many different levels—illness, childbirth, arranged marriages. There is fear and revulsion and the tremendous relief of sisterhood. Women wrote down how immense was their joy and pleasure in the less treacherous, safer confines of the like-minded. There is sheer exuberance in expressing emotion with those that understand you.

"We have, you know," said Elizabeth to the archivist, "currently substituted sex for feelings. As our use of the word 'soul' slipped away we began to believe only the physical side was gratifying. A quick fix brings with it lots of empty space in which to think about alternatives.

"The reason Henriette smiles so abundantly, so magnificently, so uninhibitedly, is because she knows she kept her soul alive."

Eva turned towards the window, noting the beautiful cascades of small luminous spiky fruits on the old horse chestnut tree, the aftermath of its candelabra flowerings.

It remade itself in its reworking of the romance of spring.

She returned to Elizabeth. "I wanted to tell you I also found an autograph. Henriette wrote a *Lebenslauf* she completed just before her death. Her last years were full of debilitating illness. She died without her vivid smile. I know you, my dear professor, are never content to just do the sums. You read between the lines.

"Now! To change the subject, my birthday party will do you no end of good. June evenings have a practical magic, Inspectors notwithstanding."

THE ONCOMING STORM

Elizabeth saw a dark line on the horizon. An ink-black line. She had only ever seen the like in the Hebrides. The horizon line where land meets the sea is key to weather prediction. Air, water and earth struggle against each other. She remembered one cloudy sky with the sun breaking through. The eerie beams of light transfigured the sea to quicksilver. Then the silver turned to a sea of lead.

In the Elbe River floodplain, the view was open on all sides. The clouds bubbled over the huge ancient trees. There were no islands like in the Hebrides as dark substantial silhouettes to break the horizon line.

Elizabeth and Eva were transporting picnic baskets and wine bottles to the gondola station. Eva nudged Elizabeth.

"You're lost in space. Come back to the present. Can you take the other handle of this carry-all? I think we can carry all the bread and salad and wine and treats to the gondola in one go."

"I was only watching the clouds," pouted Elizabeth. "The *Mitteldeutsche Zeitung* predicted a weather front coming in from the northwest. Strong winds and thunderstorms. I'm watching that enormous bank of clouds; I suppose it's a habit left over from sailing days. I always keep an eye on the weather before setting out on water."

"I think you're famished," Eva retorted, looking at the time. "The river plain has its own climate and either Berlin and/or Dresden get the downpours. Here we are prone to discount more than half of what's said in weather reports!"

Eva locked her car and picked up the handle on her side of the holdall. They had a way to go along the uneven path towards the gondola station. To their left the lake edged into the vast park, small waves making lively patterns of silver eyelets. They rippled eastwards before disappearing under the overhanging trees. In the distance the white Nymphaeum, the temple to the water spirits, stood like a toothy abandoned harp.

The two women were the first of the party to arrive. They set their burden down on a bench. As they did so, someone hailed them. None other than the Inspector, dapper and off duty. A Panama hat with a black band sat jauntily on his close-cropped hair. The collar of his wind-breaker was up, wheat-coloured over his blue shirt. He wore blue jeans, not the sloppy kind but a neatly tailored pair that showed off his muscular build.

With a start, Eva realized that though they had known each other for many years, she had never considered him in any other way than fellow city employee.

Elizabeth settled her startling straw hat with white roses and wide brim on her head and let her dress of wine red drift around what she hoped was a nicely voluptuous figure still.

"Inspector, you look fit enough to row us out into the lake!"

"No he doesn't," said Hugh, appearing on the top step leading down to the pontoon. "No-one but me is fit enough to handle those heavy oars of oak. They look like boat-yard wedges as long as an elephant's trunk, and probably as easy to manoeuvre!"

"Goodness. Who all did you invite, Eva?"

"I like foreigners," Eva's eyes twinkled. "And word travels fast among archivists. Here comes Frank from the city archives. He and his wife Martine are part of our glorious circle. They represent the best in scholarly and educational resources, not to mention Martine being an excellent cook well-known for her 'Angels-on-horseback'."

"I've brought those and raspberries from the garden,

to be indulged by all with home-made ice cream. So come and help me lift the cooler," announced Frank, keeper of the city archives. "But there has to be a joker in the pack," he added. "And here he comes."

They all turned in the direction Frank pointed. The figure moved suddenly, as if stung by a wasp, and departed in the opposite direction. Eva was incredibly relieved to see this gangly silhouette who she thought must be Wilhelm Paternoster, exit through the row of lime trees and walk towards the Woerlitz Schloss.

And, as contrast, from the opposite direction, the young Helen Brecht appeared. She had on a charcoal chunky sweater and white linen trousers and carried a huge cake. Around her shoulder on a strap hung an umbrella with a duck-beak handle. "Don't go without me," she shouted and waved.

As the official gondolier came to join them, Inspector Queberon stepped forward, saying, "I think I know you, don't I? It would be such a pleasure if you didn't mention this party at all and just filled out the papers with 'competent trained rower' and sent us off with a waterman's blessing. It's my day off."

The gondolier shrugged and gave the Inspector the key to the padlock that would release the boat.

The gondola was pushed off from the pontoon with all aboard. They spread the tablecloth out and arranged the glasses. The bread knife was laid next to the dark rye and the white wheaten loaf. Ham and salami, olives and grapes and pieces of roasted chicken were disentangled from wrappings. Fresh salad and cheese looked luscious on the long reach of the gondola's table. Bottles of wine and champagne clinked in the stern, and, up by the bow cutting into the slow tango of the waves sat the Inspector, leaning expertly into the oars. He and Hugh had reached a compromise.

Elizabeth watched for the familiar sculpture of the Shell Gatherer by the water. On land the figure seemed enormous carved in stone, her coiled hair big as your shoulders, her arms Amazonian. Across the lapping waves she was delicate, ethereal, bending down to gather the gifts of the sea. Elizabeth mused that here once more she was reminded that this landscape had an added dimension, a place where humanity supped with the gods.

There was momentary stillness as the party settled in the gondola. The Shell Gatherer receded as the boat pulled out. The heavy gondola was essentially a punt swaying on the waves, open to the winds.

On the shoreline the poplars rippled softly above the beautiful, sculpted figure, an unnatural pure white in the sinking sun's rays. The rising wind did not send a chill along her bare body. She was beyond death. Only the grasses wept, troubled, the wind making them babble. Elizabeth heard the sound and looked up to see the thickening clouds. Through them the sunset's sky-writing was more glorious than ever man could paint.

Eva handed Elizabeth her wine glass. "Weather-watching again?" she teased. "We are about to toast the slipping of all mooring ropes for this evening and, of course, my birthday! The wine is Halle-Unstrut and a Riesling, light and dry with just a hint of Elysium, the scented meadows where convivial shades, men and women of poetry and art, linger to bless the living. Professor, surely, that is territory after your own heart. And I, as archivist, can't think of better company."

Elizabeth returned her toast: "To the living and the dead, then, but enjoyment to the present company, and, mostly, from all of us, *zum Wohl* to the birthday girl! And, to quote the Polish toast to health, 'A Thousand Years.'"

They raised their glasses. Inspector Queberon's gaze was caught in the azure depths of Elizabeth's eyes. Hugh caught the fleeting, unguarded glance. His aunt, he thought, might be sailing in dangerous waters.

He raised his own glass and teased: "To all who can swim!"

"And want to wind up in a barrel of rum," countered Inspector Queberon. "Herr Knox, I think I am on the side of the angels, or whatever winged form Lord Nelson took after his heroic death. The immortal man of the telescope and the blind eye. I was in London once, squinting up at him as a statue. A seagull rose from his hat, white and majestic, soaring into the sky, replete after a hearty meal of chips. That would be the modern urban gull. Nelson, of course, never learned to swim. I unfortunately can, but I still respect the sea."

"Nelson died at sea on deck in the battle of Trafalgar," added Frank.

"He was shot and began to bleed to death and they couldn't staunch the wound. As his life ebbed, the news of victory came. What a piece of news to take with you to the afterlife! Dying in the moment of triumph, his dying of the light, but in the same moments Nelson acquired eternal fame. Around him were sinking ships of cannon-gnawed oak wood and canvas ripped and holed. The heavy smell of gunpowder stank in the nostrils and death bawled in the waves.

"They stuffed Nelson's body into a barrel of rum to keep it intact for the state funeral, that's presence of mind for you. The blood of Nelson. Such is the name of the drink," concluded Frank.

"What a drink!" added the Inspector, pulling heavily on the oars, shipping them past the silent, cloud-reflecting windows of the Prince of Anhalt-Dessau's country house.

"I only take rum in my tea," exclaimed Eva. "But Nelson was revered in Woerlitz in so many ways. Late in the day, of course. He visited this very lake with Lady

Hamilton and her tolerant husband, Sir William. Those windows staring at us witnessed the Napoleonic wars. The shifting sands of politics are ingrained in this scenery."

"Blindly looking down on us, stalwart in the gathering breeze. I'm feeling a chill," said Helen pragmatically.

The gallant Hugh stood up, taking off his windbreaker.

"They say the Scots don't feel the cold. And another glass of that sunlit Riesling will sweep the chill away." And he filled her glass.

"I was never one for hauntings, but there to our left is a flotilla. Call it the French fleet. And row on, Nelson, straight between their battle lines!"

"It's only the gondolas reserved by the hotel for an evening dinner," remarked the very sensible Martine. "They are turning back, I think, as they don't want to risk the weather worsening. But I am as romantic as the rest of you," she said, calmly observing the muscular pull on the oars and the commensurate swift glide forwards of the gondola.

"That's the test, isn't it," commented Helen. "To put away our bookish tastes and be superstitious, the light and shadows slipping things in and out of sight, and our giddy minds conjuring whatever takes fancy. Look: there rises Vesuvius. A Vesuvius in scale miniscule, but sublime. Sublime! Sublime because its presence recalls the warmth and sensuousness of the southern climes. We journey out into the Bay of Naples, the great rumbling earth a presence, the potential fires imminent. So unlike the everyday. And that's what a party is for."

Helen stood upright in the gondola. She held her glass out to the volcano positioned by design at the end of the Woerlitz lake. Her black pullover almost merged with night's darkness pulling in from the east. Hugh's windbreaker hung loose on her. The clouds were matting like fine wool. Her feet were spread to keep her balance. The partygoers looked at her youthful, graceful form, her flushed face. Hugh thought, here is a woman who *is* like a Greek goddess, who is beautiful. Am I falling in love? I'd never have thought it.

But Elizabeth thought, I tremble for her, she's going to get into trouble. The danger is much like women pulling the cork from the bottle. They have to be careful. Things are bound to overflow.

Elizabeth's gaze caught the tall spire of the church in Woerlitz, standing as upright and believing as Helen. The spire was just to the left of her. It resembled a Gothic tower with white woodwork scrolling in brilliant extravaganzas up its steeple. The steeple was modelled after a lighthouse, even having a crow's nest lookout. Here in the sea of pagan gods and temples, this Pharos blinked out its warning.

Frank held out a hand to steady Helen. He said, "Come sit down. We are a society as esoteric as the spiritualists, except our séances are held in libraries, poring over books and papers. Hedonism overtakes us when we see the object of our love, the incarnate landscapes where metaphors are real. Vesuvius travels north to sit at the end of our lake. We toast Nelson and his love, Emma Hamilton, the wife of Sir William Hamilton, the emissary and plenipotentiary of Her Majesty the Queen in the Two Kingdoms of Sicily."

Frank raised his glass once more and touched it lightly to the sparkling glass Helen in turn held out to him. All of them watched the seven gondolas of the tourist party recede and diminish as their gondoliers sought the refuge of the pontoons at the farthest end of the lake.

"Hip, Hip, Hip, Hurray!" Hugh intoned the cheer of the British Navy. They saw the fleet of clouds, shipping now in black swirling formations across the sky, and saw stretched below them that clear rim of blue, the bright sickle crescent where the eye of heaven was not yet shut and where hope still lay that the storm would pass them by.

"The toast is to conviviality, to Frank's society of romantics lost in the trackless wilds of books. What else could conjure the sparse, aesthetic Hamilton, speculator in geological theory, teetering on the bright flows of

liquid lava from the bowels of Vesuvius, and the versa-
tile Emma, dark and voluptuous, recreating the glories
of the past with her poses, the tableaux of the living
goddess, to ever get together? We see her beauty in the
portraits; we don't see the dark pools of jealous
tantrums."

"Like those swans at your back, Hugh," said Elizabeth. "They gleam an awful sinister white with their
feathers raised in that most graceful of arches, their
libidinous beaks pure red-orange. I think you had better
feed them these scraps of bread. They are coming to the
boat like a communion table, herding their cygnets to
teach them about human weakness. Sentiment has its
pitfalls."

The flotilla of swans ducked and hissed, demanding
tribute. The Inspector flicked gleaming walls of water at
them with the gondola's oars. He pushed hard and the
boat leapt between the reedy islands overgrowing the
pillars of basalt placed at the approach to the island of
Vesuvius, *The Stein,* and its assembly of buildings, the
villa Hamilton and the amphitheatre. The Inspector
banked the boat against the wooden platform. They
stepped on land, none of them quite sober.

The stones of Vesuvius gleamed in earth browns,
raw and squared. Along its cone they were bleak red
like dried blood, mixed with the ashen colours of
granite shading to bruised bluish tones. Below the

volcano on its northern flank was the spacious amphitheatre.

They climbed out of the gondola and into the protective semi-circle of the theatre. The stage was empty, a floor of stone with wisps of embattled grass perking up riotously. Beyond lay curious boulders collected by the Prince of Anhalt-Dessau as geological specimens and beyond that a dry stone wall. Scattered widely throughout were *Kaiserkerzen*, a more beautiful name than Great Mullein, with its allusion to tall candles meant for the emperor. These were taller than a child and had soft spear-shaped leaves opening to tapering yellow flowers on their spires. It was as if all was lit by their yellows while the ardent blues of Cranesbills and cornflowers littered the island wantonly.

The wind had dropped and for the time it took the party to climb the tiered rock, they imagined themselves sole inhabitants of the earth.

Martine thought they were like small puppets scrambling on the circular seating that made up the theatre. Most of the party sat facing the empty stage. Who might take it? Here was an assembly that knew not so very much about each other, but a great deal about the past. She was sitting alone higher up, watching.

Each man and woman here could pin dates and people involved in the past on a very precise historical map. They were experts in historical excavation. An interesting point, Martine observed, as they had not ventured to an actual archaeological site, but only its copy, its reincarnation as earth-worship, really. The volcano sat brooding, its cone angled into the sky. She thought it foreboding with its dark upward slanted snout.

It was the symbol of uncontrollable fiery forces that shaped the crust of the earth. They were no different from Sir William Hamilton laboriously climbing the flanks of the great volcano, in love with his fields of fire, gathering every morsel of knowledge about his temperamental beloved. He wanted to know the secrets of the earth. He wanted it secularized, he wanted the biblical floods to recede, to no more impede the great science of geology; he wanted fire to be the leaven that formed and pressed upwards the mighty, surly folds of hill and mountain. He was a gaunt visionary.

Martine, as one of the librarians of the Wissentschafliche Bibliothek and friend to Emma Specht, knew well the beautiful hand-coloured copper plates in Hamilton's famous book. He was included there as a dark shadow illuminated from behind by the red hot lava flow curling past his feet, his thin rod of a walking stick angled away from his body as he leaned forward.

Martine looked down on this small convocation of

librarians, archivists, historians, and the oddly included Inspector. They were like inebriated musicians come to make music in the hallowed ruins of eighteenth-century ideas. They plucked strings in a melody that invoked strange composites—memory and symbol, voices, ghosts, theories, careers.

Inspector Queberon, the odd man out, stood to speak.

"Let us raise our glasses to Eva Delamotte and to another fine year of her presence here in Dessau. I owe her many a good tip as an amateur sleuth. I myself love history! I am honoured to be in your company. And I spill a libation to the ghosts assembled with us: the Prince, the Admiral, the Ambassador, and Ladies Past and Present."

Helen shivered. The glint in Queberon's eye under the skewed Panama was like a sickle mowing summer grass. There was a hint of Hogarth's rake about him.

And she had never seen the elegant Eva tipsy. The cold volcano made the false heat of drink desirable. Then there were the ghosts, the flickering thoughts of sensuous Emma whirling slowly in her scant clothing, the eyes of Hamilton watchful. Lord Nelson, a gambler in sea engagements, could be seen drowning in the voluptuous, cresting waves of desire pulling him in the wake of such an accomplished concubine. The currents of sea and political power, the volcanic subconscious, were coursing this lodestone of transported landscape, this northern-most, this Bay of Naples.

She looked towards the enigmatic nephew and aunt, the Celtic imports. Drink was put away properly by them. They were used to it. It no doubt genetically coursed in the guts of the muscular handsome features of Hugh, who gave nothing away. She did not, after all, know him at all well.

The erudite and untouchable Elizabeth Hammerstein sat with her legs beautifully crossed, her face flushed. Would Dessau lift this impenetrable mask? Helen knew her well enough to know she cared dearly about the women she wrote about. She found that laudable. But the dead were never at rest when disturbed. They had their own agendas.

Lord Nelson was dead too, but had a great reputation. And his alter ego—Martine was very sober—yes, the police Inspector, was as handsome as his hero in his inscrutable masculinity.

So many ghosts and the wind rising.

The wind sang lugubriously, panting through the orifices of rock, the porous, dirt-red iron ore and the impenetrable granites. The island of imported stone and artifice turned darker.

Elizabeth glanced at the trees bending to the wind and saw the clouds like anvils advancing. This was surely the storm—and it had not passed them by.

Snatching picnic things and wraps, they made for the gondola like chickens to the roost. The mooring ties were loosened and the Inspector bent his strength to the oars. The gondola creaked forward, waves lapping noisily against the hull. In minutes the universe had changed, the benign mask of nature slipping to show her ferocious power.

A roaring wind bent branches under its might. The spot-lit *Schloss* quavered like a mirage far away. The tall reeds lining the lake bent, then surged upright, hissing. The Inspector's hat flew off as if guillotined, and sped, cartwheeling, into the lake. Elizabeth's floral summer extravagance followed suit, drowned in engulfing waters. The napkins rose and left the ship like rats.

Out of the corner of his eye, while pulling hard towards shore, Inspector Queberon caught sight of a hull that shouldn't have been there at all. It came from his left, at the entrance to the Wolf Canal. The boat had a powerful diesel engine on full throttle. Its prow aimed at them as if it would run them down.

Helen held Martine's hand as long spears of light stabbed down, followed by loud rolls of thunder. Hugh and Frank pulled their collars up. Eva was stiff with fear. Then Elizabeth shrieked against the storm's noise, pointing at the v-shaped wave of the black power-boat making for the gondola. A shot rang out.

The screech of metal clawing wood put everything

out of mind. The picnic gondola swerved. It had been pushed hard by a mighty force, but this inscrutable spear of a motorboat had turned swiftly in the dark and disappeared, leaving startled passengers tipped every which way.

The gondola hit the moored ferry parked in the lake just in front of the pontoons. The gondola listed, over-turning as everyone jumped over the side. The wet cold water pooled in. The clammy intimacy of soaked clothes coiled around Elizabeth's body. And then fell the torren-tial rain, mixed with hailstones.

Elizabeth's last impression was of wave upon wave of shimmering light. But she was determined to breathe. Her instinct was to gain air, to resurface. She must swim. She fought to swim.

She slapped Inspector Queberon across the face as she moved into her crawl stroke. He instinctively caught her wrist, wrenched her under. Then he must have realised he was drowning her. He moved close. His body was very powerful. She felt its length. They pulled to the surface simultaneously, merman and mermaid. The black water broke in endless distending rings around them.

Frank was hauling Martine to the grassy shore. She sat down, wet and shaking, her drenched clothes clinging.

The Inspector too reached shore and waded out

again. Elizabeth was close behind. She turned, exhausted, to look for the others. The rain was pelting down by now, dancing in gusts.

There were three floating bodies, all with their heads down. One was close, and recognizable as the elegant, gaunt form so familiar from countless, smiling encounters. The other two bodies were male, young, and equally lifeless.

With one leap Elizabeth was in the water, pulling in a fast crawl towards Eva. She had learned how to rescue at sea as a lifeguard in her teens. She flipped the body over, managed to secure a hold; towed with a powerful stroke. On land Frank took over, pumping life back in, using his first-aid skills.

The Inspector, too, jumped, swum madly, hooked the other body, and towed it to shore.

Elizabeth was shocked as the sullen, sodden flesh was heaved on land, face upwards. If it was Hugh she would never forgive herself, never come here again. Hugh, of course, could not swim, despite his taunting the Inspector.

She nearly fainted with relief, hurt her wrist as she sank on the grass. The face was not Hugh, but contorted, its lines frozen in bizarre wrinkles. The hands had on odd white gloves. She remembered him gesturing in the library. There was a leaking hole in his chest, water and blood oozing out. The body was clown-like, twisted.

Night had set in. Elizabeth looked blankly into the dense rain again. Her head drummed with adrenalin and her body shook with hypothermia. She stood up and turned and there like figments of her imagination, two more figures stumbled down the slope. One was a wet black bear with flowing locks. The other hung this form over his shoulder. He was a slim rake of a young man, dripping water. She recognized Hugh. Helen's pullover was a sodden bear's pelt, but a thin crescent of a smile played on the she-bear's lips.

A moment later Elizabeth heard the authoritative voice of Queberon. "That's Dr. William Paternoster shot through the heart," said the Inspector.

All eyes travelled to the squid-like corpse, sprawled on the dank grass, eyes still open, the rain running like tears, unstoppable, over his white eyeballs, staring eyes, the slow and cold finality of his bland face.

AFTERLIFE

"**O**h God," said Hugh, coming to again in the arms of Helen after he had rescued her—or was it the other way round?

Helen was shivering. She'd dumped her heavy black jumper and it lay like a dung heap on the ground. They thought they saw a light; then it went out. The next beam was blinding, a set of headlights from a police car bumping up the track to the gondola station. It caught them like figures in a film, wretched soldiers trudging from a fierce engagement.

Frank and Martine helped them, practical and kind with the weary Hugh and the exhausted Helen. Everywhere else there was milling about.

Paternoster was sent on his way to the morgue.

. . .

STARS ARE the saintly eyes of night. Their twinkling curiosity inhabits the velvety black, restoring the sanctuary of heaven. Far away the baroque curve of dwindling cloud shot through with umber-violet flashes receded. Inspector Queberon walked in the stillness left behind. The soft clarity of night brushed sweetly across his wearied face.

Tiredness made him single-minded. "Go back," he thought, "to that moment the world went flat." He ruminated further, but sharply. "It was a single shot. And it could not have come from over the water. No marksman alive could aim with such precision when underway in a boat at speed," and, he added, "the aim would have had to be very steady and with night-assisted vision. The murderer could have stood anywhere here or near the house, a place public and discreet all at the same time."

He came to the lawn in front of the yellow glow of Corinthian columns. The wan starlight was diffused farther out between the plantings in the patchwork of the dark. The windows glittered.

Queberon was surprised to feel his heart lurch with foreboding. He began to systematically search the many silvered and shadowed hidey-holes of night. He saw the memorial urn on its pedestal with its rhythmic runnels like the folds in a tunic. Then he looked over to the house. In the middle distance he saw a clutch of darkness deeper than the night. Its buxom form reminded him of someone he knew. She was swathed in rain clothes.

EVER SINCE SHE crawled ashore and had assured Queberon she had not drowned, Eva followed the sheen on the border of water and shore. Somewhere was a car park. But she was missing it. It was like a storyline, the silvery voice of Scheherazade, the lure of night.

She stumbled along the lake, the tingling of her skin as the night winds dried her giving the sensation she might be a fabled creature risen from the deep. It was as if she had left behind her the life of her ordinary self.

Entranced, she saw before her the shifting cloud-scapes moving westwards, the caravans of the night. The cone of Vesuvius bayed into the dark like a wolf. Her numbed senses caught the prick of the moon emerging again and again from the clouds. It was a dream. Her wet clothes hung like Greek drapery over her slim arms, her slight hips and narrow breasts. The shimmer of light from the Prince's Palladian mansion, its ever-present illumination, fell on the pleasant arch of the small pavilion called the English Seat.

Here, it seemed to Eva, was the gateway to the other-world, the sanctuary where she could rest. She would converse with the Shades. She would slough her mind of books and enquiries, of rationality and the will to live. She would be winged and become an angel like a bird with very fine feathers. They would be white, untouched by any smirch of earthly desire. She would rise into the stars.

She saw the path angle upwards towards this gentle heavenly Seat. Nothing mattered, but that she would lay her smooth limbs on that cool stone seat. Her footsteps took her upwards.

Until the enraged swan reached her. They are huge when the white arcs of feathers beat their drum of annoyance and deep displeasure. The warrior swan rushed from the inlet, long white neck out, red beak parted, hissing with territorial rage.

Adrenalin rushed Eva back to the present. She felt her bruises, her wet hair, and her broken nails from her crawl up the banks. The swan's attack was painful. He hacked at the back of her thighs with his beak, biting her. The beauties of night evaporated in the more practical need to escape the bird. She ran awkwardly up the path, no longer travelling the road to Elysium.

She had plonked back into the mundane. She knew now where the car park was.

OTHERWORLDLY LADIES

The gondola lay like half-eaten cake crumbled into the milky latte of the rain-foamed lake. The shards of broken wine glasses glittered forlornly. Strawberries swam like tropical fish in the salad bowl. An oar splayed like an injured flipper. Then curtains of rain began to shroud it all as if the show was finally over.

Elizabeth wound her way past the illuminated façade of the Prince of Anhalt-Dessau's house, the Corinthian pillars of its portico gilded, exotic, everything fronded now with searchlights.

Beneath the portico's roof Elizabeth knew that the signs of the Zodiac loomed, copied from the Temple of Bel, the reigning Idol of the Sun, in Palmyra, a million thought-centuries away. The gravelled path cut into her feet. She had lost her shoes.

Frank had stayed, while Martine had sprinted for help and warm blankets. The Inspector had overtaken Martine running towards the hotel, a fit man, now mentally back in uniform. Helen and Hugh were with Frank.

That left Elizabeth to recollect alone. Shock dulled her senses. The cold was actually a blessing. Her icy skin made her move, reminded her she was walking in the here and now, that in near five minutes the blazing lights of the nearest hotel lobby would come into view.

Her mind was still awash with the feel of water as she had opened her eyes to its murky world of indistinct space, her panicked struggle to surface, to break the barrier of death, to come back into existence, to escape the hold of undercurrents, those slow-moving veils of vague, enclosing murk. Like her heartbeat her trained mind absorbed this knowledge, this ticker-tape message that she had almost succumbed.

Something had shot out of the recesses of the canal that eventually led past the temple of Venus. That leaping power-boat lunged and seemed to push her under even now. And it had pushed the gondola towards its collision.

Her knees buckled at the memory. She collapsed on the grass. She had taken the path towards a pavilion to the right of the main house. Normally one could go through the glass doors there and reach the restaurant on the other side. The large windows were marked with mercurial smears from the reflected illumination of Schloss Woerlitz. She struggled to sit up. To regain her independence. She looked up. And she was startled.

Directly in her line of vision was what she had passed so often and not thought about. This was the small altar that hid a well. The chiselled face that turned towards her from the side of the altar was one she knew, the profile of the moon goddess, Selene, arising from the crescent, and next to her the effigy of the carved morning star, the torch being down-turned, signifying the encroaching night. Elizabeth's gaze lifted upwards.

There stood a lady wearing a white dress of centuries ago. Her ethereal gown was floating in the rain. Her one arm lent on the altar and gently propped up her head. Her head was veiled in gauzy white. Her enormous, gentle eyes rested on Elizabeth. And then the silvery threads of light from the illuminated house caught the pavilion windows and she was gone.

But what impressed Elizabeth was the look of kindness cast toward her; it was fleeting, but strongly expressive of concern. The ghostly lady was keeping track of her.

Elizabeth sank down on the clammy grass. Her

aching body succumbed to its fatigue. The rain came
sweeping down on her, a balm of sisterly annihilation.

INSPECTOR QUEBERON SAT in the hotel manager's office
getting the homicide investigation underway. He was in
control, that singular switch in the brain that comes
with his kind of job kicking in all the energy he still
possessed.

"We've got forensic out there," said the policeman
responsible. "The victim collapsed on the bank, shot
through the heart. Not a complicated murder. And we're
looking for the speedboat you said you'd seen. But, as
you know the park is dark as black velvet. And the rain
is eroding the canal edges. Speedboats can be very fast
and elusive."

"What about Paternoster?" asked Queberon.

"A minor academic with the History Department at
the University of Halle. No criminal record, as of the
latest computer check. Early days, though."

"Not easy taking aim from a speeding boat. Just one
try, too. To my mind the shot must have come from
elsewhere. But that's another issue. Have you been able
to find out where the speedboat came from?"

"Inspector," said his subordinate, "even with Dessau a
quiet town and losing population like dew on a hot day,
we have a rich zoo to pick from, not counting the

keepers in Berlin or Halle; even the sharks in Roslau, come to think of it."

Queberon had to laugh.

"You mean our sister city on the Elbe, passed in the blink of an eye? Sure, they have a boat shed and nice harbour and immediate access to the river in Rosslau. But so do we, by the way, that very same access. And if you're talking speedboats, Dessau has its own harbour. That innocent looking boatyard like the blunt nose of a sheep jutting in from the Elbe is where we keep the water police busy. They have a large shiny shed on floats. But other boats tie up at that quay too. And then there are the acres and acres of sandy river beaches. Not discounting the disused pontoons down-river for the pleasure boats that don't dock there anymore."

"Inspector, we shall start with the innumerable hide-outs and landing places—we have enough local police to see to our inquiries! I'll see to it! But as we track them all down, remember that the one murder here and now remains of vital concern. This single corpse.

"In this case we have history man, as you said, shot by a pro. We have the rain removing the evidence. Paternoster was wearing those strange white gloves they use to read valuable old books with, by the way. He still has his spectacles on his nose with raindrops on them. They were pointing up, as he collapsed backwards, and the lightning in Coswig inscribed them; lightning ran like spiders across his glasses. The storm passed north."

"It's all so bloody peculiar," remarked Queberon. "A loose cannon from the ships of academia rolling on the dark deck of a fine landscape garden on a fine summer evening. I thought the Interdisciplinary Centre for the Study of the Enlightenment slept peacefully at night."

"Who knows what their dreams are? We're only responsible for law and order, not the crimes of lecturing. The thing academics are good at is snooping, unearthing what others thought lost in time. Which leads me to surmise Paternoster must have known something worth more than scribbles on paper.

"Now, the door to the Woerlitz Schloss was open, the one under the stairs leading to the portico. Any number of people have keys: cleaners; curators; those doing restoration work; even the head honcho, the beloved Direktor Eszett. What was out of the ordinary were very wet footsteps, slightly oily, on the stairs leading to the top offices, those rooms above the ones open to tourists."

"You mean the ones with the lithographs of famous sea battles and of the Admirals of the British Navy? And the desks of visiting researchers gathering notes on the Prince of Anhalt-Dessau's domains?" said Queberon. "That depository of the first naval empire's glories and key to Dessau's anglophilia? *That* had footprints?"

"Like from a crow's nest in the rigging, if that's a sound metaphor, an accurate shot could have been fired, especially through crosshairs. Both from the speedboat or from the top floor. Better concentrate now on the oily, watery footsteps on the stairs and these, I'm telling you, were too small for a man's boots."

ELIZABETH'S CHEEK was nestled in the bent grass. As her conscious mind ebbed, the rivers of the imagination grew with the incoming tide of new imagery. She was trying to recover, but uncertainty had taken hold of her.

The figure she had seen leaning against the altar of the moon walked towards her. She saw the robust features, the strong chin and the large eyes, the tall shape, regal but also weighed down, displaying a motion careworn, tentative.

The vision walked through Elizabeth's huddled body, a cool passage of wind, down the path towards the lake and raised her arm in a fond greeting. Coming from the other direction was Henriette, a slim, graceful woman, her hair tied back, the modest curls falling forward around her neck. Her eyes were sky blue and shone. In the form of an arc of pleasurable friendship, the lips tipped upwards at both corners. She didn't need to speak. The radiance of her face spoke for her.

The two women embraced. Then the vision faded into darkness.

Elizabeth felt she saw the light empty from between the trees, from the glittering expanses of water. Darkness slipped over her and obliterated rational thinking.

She succumbed to the struggle to reach the lights of a police car. Finally, dreadfully, she no longer moved. Her inert body lay curled in foetal regression on the wet lawn.

Coming from the path that lead down from beyond the Summer Pavilion was an incongruous figure. Swathed in rain gear, water pearling along its waxed surface, the seam of it nearly down to the low-heeled boots, a sou'wester hat as black as soot, its rims low like the petals of a nasturtium, obscuring the face, and a beam of tight electric light shining on the water-splurged path, she advanced decisively.

Babylonia von Moritzburg wanted no-one and nothing to cross her path. She knew her way and thought she would extinguish the torch, but the path itself was slippery. Her boots were too fashionable for it, really. And she was already too hot under the English Barbour with its bulging pockets. Better to fall, than be detected.

Her foot squelched on the rim of a particularly large puddle. She stopped to go around, mindful that her expensive leather boots were thin and she liked them.

She might wear them again as proof of her audacity. She flicked her torch on, sideways, to keep clear of mud and the pools of water. The light swerved on the grass, catching the huddled form of Elizabeth Hammerstein.

It took her only a moment to decide. The Good Samaritan was always a spooky figure she had detested in her elite upbringing. Why waste time on someone else's destiny?

And dead was certainly dead. Probably better for humanity that these academics were eradicated. They caused no end of obfuscation. This one looked dowdier than ever in her wet clothing. Let the dead bury the dead.

TURNING THE PAGE

Babylonia leant back onto her pillows, surrounded by the soft expanse of fine linen. People always misjudged her. Money was such a delicious thing.

What was the point if one looked ragged when young? She was young, or in her prime, at least. Nothing wrinkly around the eyes or that upper lip. Everything plump and well-fed, edible really, and she felt an electric pleasure at her womanly power. Pity the scrawny, she thought.

Eszett would be easy prey. She toyed with the shot of whisky on her bedside table. She brought the Johnnie Walker to her lips, the hot searing pleasure dribbling down her throat. Let the rain make others miserable elsewhere. Here she was safe in the soft cocoon of her butterfly beauty; here in these sheets she felt luxurious.

The sheer cupidity of men, like that Paternoster, idling up to her like a car's hot breath when it rode next to the kerb, wanting to please, wanting to cruise right up to her, tell her he'd found the evidence to her claim on part of the Woerlitz estate.

He had offered research, genealogical expertise! Her entitlement to a good portion of land just beyond that knob of a thing called the Vesuvius.

He had successfully found the last will and testament of both Henriette and Albrecht. They appeared as separate items in the Wissenschaftliche Bibliothek and the archive. Paternoster knew where they were, how to join them up, and who to name as beneficiary. There would be no doubt about the succession or Babylonia's claim.

She could build a luxury hotel there, lots of units with views out over the lake, and some swimming pools thrown in, but exclusive. She would market it with one of the best chefs in the land called in to provide that other luxury, exquisite concupiscence.

She knew her moneyed friends. Nothing like top quality wine and seriously exceptional food. And then she would work on Direktor Eszett for exclusive access to the gondolas and monuments. She would have them lit up with beeswax candles, giving everything that false ghostly glow that the antique required. She liked the idea of the rocks below the Vesuvius inundated with candlelight.

She'd see to it that in the Pantheon there would be a party with a few salacious tableaux thrown in, nothing too obvious, but then, the erotic element was never too far from the pagan. And that would be fine among the Muses.

All she needed were those title deeds, or at least her proven entitlement and that thanks to Paternoster. She was the last in line.

She crowed over that stupid Paternoster with his flapping ears. They had stood out slightly from his head and in silhouette. They gave perfect markers for her crosshair sights. A black shadow with pot-handle lugs. A man like an Etruscan vase, all convoluted mind and no ingredients, nothing going on below the waist. And a shot through the heart would be easy.

She had him in one shot. He squirmed like a rabbit, fell, twitched. The Muses wouldn't miss him, and neither would she.

ELIZABETH SURFACED into swaying thought as if she were putting behind her a starlit blackness in which she lost all her bearings. At first she thought the single light that shone on her must be the crescent moon. She was not entirely sure. But it was the reading lamp, slightly aslant by the side of her bed.

There was a humming and spiralling in and out of the crescent light that was forming words; slow-to-surface words, words that swam upwards. She tried to locate herself in this coming and going of shadows, the light swaying invitingly like light reflected in water and the words seemed like they were runes floating. She was giving up; then again she wasn't. She was diving in and out of despair.

The first word she caught was 'night'. Then she fished for another—'arrest'. Did it mean 'stop'? Or was she catching the coattails of 'criminal'? The moon swam by and she managed 'Q' as in 'O', full, with a small tail, a coda, a comma, a hanging thread.

Elizabeth's eyes opened at last and began to focus. There was this figure sitting by her bed. At first she thought: the goddess Isis, clad in black, robed fulsomely. Had the moon goddess risen with her from the black waters of the churned lake? The goddess among whose attributes was the realm of storm. Isis, Queen of the Heavens, veiled and hidden, imparting death or life?

Only the muscles of the goddess were not at all heavenly; they were too thick, she thought. Then she thought: I have pain, icy runs of pain and a headache. This is not death: it is the misery of life.

Beyond was her celestial comforter, the bedside lamp, and beyond this, she realized slowly, sat Inspector Queberon. He had noticed her movement. He tentatively reached out to touch her hand lying on the coverlet.

Words fail me, she thought. There are no words except the ones that escape from the cold, muddy depths. But there is no sea kelp in the lake. The kelp forests begin in the sea. The great reaching-out limbs of green, floating kelp, so easy, so used to the tides of coming and going.

She was coming and going in very different places. Sometimes she thought, I am at home.

The cold sea of the West Coast. That land of bareness except for the ice-white quartz lines of writing through it; the wet, shining white in the basalt rock. I might want to see it. I might go there and take that warm sliver of a human hand with me.

Why, she didn't know, but she moved her thin hand to grasp it. It seemed a hook of light, a light-line, a smile of warmth. Flesh is like that, she thought. It reflects the mind.

She came to. She realized she must turn the page, be brave and accomplish her study of women's history: telling their story was her life's mission.

IT HAD BEEN in the early hours with the lawn spangled

with dew when Queberon had found Elizabeth. He was examining the area around the lake once more. He had seen the wet clothing in a heap and it had given off a faint pearling gleam; that had lured him, just as the dawn pushed over the calm surface of the lake. He was drawn to her. He did his duty. But was there more?

RECOLLECTION

Eva straightened her spine. She was sitting in the deep shadow of the English Seat, a Palladian sanctuary, much out of breath. The horde of swans had tired of their chase and now she would have to walk barefoot and tell the archive she was still alive—and that on her birthday.

She marvelled at herself, shivering like an adolescent after a skinny-dip. And her past life crowded in because there was no defence against it in her exhaustion. It marched beside her, the lean years and the fat, like a caravan from the Orient.

A mirage, she thought, but weighty. Weren't all 'trains of thought' highly charged caravans receding along the silk road into the mysterious Orient of the past?

Her mother, Maxine, still elegant in her nineties, was shrunken like a fairy, with the tiniest of hands and feet, tiaras forever perched in her snowy hair. Max, her father, a man tall and thin and silent, offspring of Westphalia's dourest legal dynasty, had been ever careful, forever pointing out the devil in the detail.

She had made top grades, never missed her classes. Sat with her parents in café and *Konditorei*. Opulence wafted from the chocolate cakes and the rum-doused almond tart, smell of roasted coffee swirling.

Oh but her feet were hurting on the sharp pebbles. She craved a black, sweet coffee. The semi-light of the *Schloss* shone through the shrubbery, making uneven zebra patterns on the grass.

In Münster, too, the castles had been lit at night, but they were late baroque with curlicue ornaments like whipped cream and a trumpet or two held by angels. Then there were the ditches or rather the defensive moats filled by fathomless murky water, like chastity belts around the proud castle walls. These landmark bulwarks of the gentry had brooded over her childhood, her very proper upbringing.

She looked down at her tattered, bedraggled self and laughed. She had chosen, rotten birthday or not. She was in every sense an archivist, even in detecting murder and motive. She would be her own woman.

RECONNAISSANCE

Inspector Queberon spun the night out into the morning, tapping in numbers on his mobile, calling in forensics, the photographer, and reinforcements.

Wreckage and trampled grass, slug trails of sliding boots, and mud and ever deeper puddles marked the scene of the crime. Ripples were left behind whenever someone splashed through the shore. The waters crisscrossed and became derogatory grinning mouths.

Alexander Pope, Inspector Queberon mused, would have let loose rhymed satires on the spirit of place. He would have squinted at the sky in his turbaned head, pointing his ghostly walking stick towards the Thames while remarking that skiffs and merchant vessels forever plied rivers to their advantage.

Queberon went on thinking. The shot could not have come from the boat. And no-one in that fast-moving boat could have fired a gun because it had come towards the gondola at full speed. No-one could have steered such a boat, caused such damage, and completed a well-aimed shot at the same time. Someone truly dexterous had aimed a missile of diesel—that would be the speedboat—through the storm at the gondola and escaped. But whoever steered the boat could not have aimed the gun.

And yet despite the damage, in a bizarre gesture, the forensic crew had found a white marzipan birthday cake with unlit red-striped candles smack in the middle by the central seat of the rescued gondola. *Happy Birthday Inspector* was written in red liquorice on the pristine white marzipan.

Between the malice aforethought that wrecked the gondola and the gunshot that murdered Paternoster through the heart, there seemed to be no connection. And, of course, it was not *his, the Inspector's* birthday, but that of Dr. Delamotte. Maybe the finely baked birthday cake was placed prominently in the aftermath of all the trouble to serve as a warning—specifically to Queberon.

"The patisserie cooks," Alexander Pope whispered in the Inspector's ear, "bear watching. Behind every successful man there is a good cook."

The cake was an English fruitcake with the de

rigueur heavy, sweet marzipan so unlike the real almond paste used on the Continent. It was certainly not an amateur cake. "Here's a tell-tale sign," whispered Pope, ever the wise ghost. "Hell hath no fury like ... a pastry cook."

Inspector Queberon looked up. Approaching him was a tall figure. It seemed like an emissary from a land of magic with very strange clothes. It was dripping water. But it was just a very breathtakingly sea-doused woman.

Her sensuous form was moulded in the voluptuousness of wet clothing sticking like Greek drapery to her lithe body.

Inspector Queberon's eyes widened. Alexander Pope vanished in an innocent white cloud.

TOUCH WOOD

All alone, recuperating in the Eyserbeck House, Elizabeth was deeply in thought. She had surfaced with a longing for the Celtic island of her birth. Nearly drowning had its impact. She needed time to recuperate and to consider.

"What better method than a slow ride through the woods on a bicycle!"

She lay back and projected her possibilities. "When I am once more settled in my accommodation in the Eyserbeck House, I will set out and just view the summer trees and wild flowers growing. I won't think for a while. And then I'll be fit for anything!"

She surveyed her lodgings, happy just to breathe the air of oaks and pines and look towards the bright presence of the Luisium.

From her window, she eyed the small cars driven by those who could barely afford them, the waitresses and cooks. The young who had all the joy of the use of their limbs, drove their vehicles into the courtyard between the house she rented and the Orangerie restaurant. These cars were tired old things, cluttering the courtyard even though the rules of the garden were explicit in banning them.

She took a deep breath and exhaled slowly. "I know the story of the Orangerie and by reciting it, I will be ever wiser and calmer. Long ago, this Orangerie here housed the rare specimens of the citrus family that gardeners tweaked and cozened as rarities in these northern climes," she began, concentrating on history as a force for temporarily focussing on 'the other'.

"It was modelled on the Orangery in Kew built by Sir William Chambers. Here in the Luisium gardens it was used, as indeed it was now also in Kew, as a restaurant.

"That is why there is such a gathering of white-frocked cooks in the courtyard opposite."

THE EYSERBECK HOUSE had a door handle in the form of a small dragon.

Elizabeth carefully stroked its puckered back and long nose, shutting the door. She wanted to go out and reconsider the many mishaps that had turned her life into such a difficult noose to escape.

She swung herself into the saddle of her bicycle despite all the challenges in her way. She pedalled along the cobbles in the courtyard, happy to be in motion, eyeing the jaunty tub of begonias in startling pink placed on the old wooden lid of the well next to a pump handle that was placed half-way up its water pipe.

If pumped hard it would recall a past benefit to hot steaming coach horses and work done by hand, the manual labour involved in tending the gardens, the horses, the fetch and carry of court life, the many servants that came and went with Louise.

The bicycle crunched hard dirt and chipped stones away as Elizabeth gathered speed. She wheeled past the Luisium in its luminous cubic form on her left and through the white pillared gateway. She was then on the sightline cut straight north from the hunting lodge, the house that had stood in the river meadows and forests before the new Luisium was built, now so long ago.

This was a route Elizabeth loved. As she peddled north the beautiful yellow double cube with its small lantern-room top receded, becoming a mere gleam in the enveloping high trees until it looked a doll's house, ever tinier and more mysterious. She occasionally looked back to see along the dusty track the pale as moth's wings house diminish to where the pyramid roof seemed to draw all of nature towards itself, a hieroglyph of beauty.

The house was lost to view as she turned west towards the River Mulde. She was making for the wooden bridge that would carry her over its fast-flowing waters and onto the cycle path to the Georgium, the landscape garden built for Louise's brother-in-law, Hans George.

The wind ruffled her hair and brought sweet smells, ripe and earthy. She felt liberated, free at last of the dark shadow of the car crash and the terrible accident with the gondola.

True to how she was appreciating her new role in speaking not just of findings, but with conviction, she heard the rustle of wind in the oaks, a whispering and lulling sound the people of past times had said were the trees talking.

The oaks were the souls of those who had lived here and entered the sap rising every spring. They conjoined their voices with the sweet susurrations of wind and leaves.

The early summer had been warm and rainy so the leaves grew in their millions, a dark waxy green, lobed as if the Green Man had bitten them and found them delicious, recommending their taste to the sprites of the winds.

The rustling winds, Elizabeth thought, were gleefully

engaged in tossing this healthy woodland. The oak soli-
taires were as big as thunderclouds and the sky was a
blue salad bowl. All their branches reached out to the
very ground where the summer grasses joined them in
waving benignly in the sun.

"I will gather my energies to trace Louise and Henriette—the models for women's friendship—and I'll make
sure that audiences, historians, cooks, librarians, and the
police—whoever—take note." And she shouted with joy.

The gentle speed at which she rode let the countryside slip by in rich and gentle summer vistas. The
motion made for her complete pleasure. She imagined
herself a butterfly on a bicycle.

She cycled by the water—watching it mirror clouds
and trees, trees and clouds. What were books compared
to nature? To stop. To look. To cycle. To replenish the
soul.

She passed the Elbe Pavilion. The forest fell away
and the streets of Dessau began again.

CATS' PAWS

A cat's mind is inscrutable. On earth at least, if not in heaven.

That was not exactly what Hugh thought, but then as he rounded the corner of the Eyserbeck House, he was looking for his aunt, not for cats. He couldn't avoid them, however.

Here there were two. One of these toy tigers raised his naked claws and then, uncoiling, sprang forwards, his tail whiplashing behind him. The evening light ignited his sleek fur to flickering embers. The other cat was the colour of angels, pure white, a fluffed-out colour that was immune to darkness.

What strange animals, Hugh thought, in a perfectly ordinary setting.

This   second   cat   too   sprang   forward,   paws

outstretched. He sprang in lithesome arcs, alert, ears pricked. Had his prey been an injured bird the claws would have rent it, broken its feathers and maimed a sojourner of the skies to death.

Hugh was taken aback as he stood transfixed in the courtyard that stretched between the Eyserbeck House and the Orangerie restaurant.

He saw the big white cat jump up on the green door of one of the storage rooms. He seemed to claw air, fell to the ground, and sprang again. Next, the slinky grey cat did the same. They seemed maniacal. Then they became distracted and ran in a beeline towards Hugh.

He had been using a crutch ever since the gondola crash and was nervous about the two cats between his feet. He stood stock still. Their ears cocked skyward and their whiskers scanned their next passage. The feline predators leapt towards him. Then they flipped like surfers.

Hugh was at a loss as to what made the cats scramble and pounce. It was a silent pantomime of chase and kill.

There was a sudden raucous laugh to his left. A man tall as a rake with a thatch of black hair and drooping eyes turned towards him. "I make them chase a laser beam. All air and no substance. Look closely and a small illuminated dot of light runs ahead of my cats. It keeps them alert. They love the chase."

This man was a novelty to Hugh. "I didn't know anyone else stayed here except my aunt," he said.

The man looked at Hugh and smirked. "Moonshine is what my cats are after. All I have to do is beam that laser point. Then they go for it, even up the walls! Been in an accident, my friend? Maybe you would feel better using an electric wheelchair. Beats that crutch."

Hugh coughed. "Hardly worth mentioning. Can't drive anywhere, though. Caught my right foot and injured it … uh … running. Nice when you get offered extra pieces of good chocolate cake, though, because people feel sorry for you. Germany has really good cooks, particularly pastry cooks."

"Used to be an expert pastry cook myself," said the man, calling to his cats Fritz and Clausewitz. "They're neutered but I like to give them the kick of Prussian special names. Fritz is obvious. And Clausewitz was one of the first theorists of war."

The two cats sat with a peculiar smile running like wizard's laughter right up to their cheeks and their red tongues patted their upturned mouths. Old Fritz lifted his paw over his eyebrow whiskers as if surveying battlefields against the decadent Austrians. Clausewitz started doing manoeuvres for outflanking the enemy by rolling on his back. His tail lashed ominously as the tall black-haired man held out a morsel of food.

"Cooks are the life-blood of every nation. You are

what you eat. A Beefeater is what you look like; pretty English." And he smiled like his cats.

"Rather along the lines of porridge oats with salt," countered Hugh deprecatingly. "I'm Scottish."

"Rangers or Celtic?" said the cook, whose name was Manfred Broadford.

"Bonnie Prince Charlie," said Hugh with a dangerous glint in his eye.

"Is that volleyball or whisky?" said Manfred, the cook and pastry specialist.

"Pure malt," said Hugh, and stroked Clausewitz who was eyeing him through green-eyed slits, but purring.

OLD FRITZ always slunk when entering a house. His innocent angel's fluff hair stood on end and he furtively extended his paws as if they had riding boots on. This had earned him his name, as his master the cook had once gone to the Brunswick Museum in which were displayed the worn riding boots of Frederick the Great, elegant, wrinkled and of the finest leather. With a splash of imagination the cook had envisioned the King of Prussia on the ground before that great ascent into the saddle. All greatness has its feet of clay.

Clausewitz, on the other hand, was nimble. So convinced of his prowess was he that he landed solidly among the framed pictures on the drinks cupboard and caused them to cascade. Their falling thunder made the tall man hurry inside.

The delightful photograph of Babylonia in a cook's white hat, much like a mushroom in its pure white, and wielding a spatula, lay cracked on the floor. He blew her a kiss and stood the picture back up, despite it now having a jagged crack like lightning right through it. He had enjoyed teaching his course Celebrities and Cooks in a top Berlin hotel. Babylonia, he remembered with a hot flash in his groin, had smacked her lips and drawn them slowly over the wooden cooking spoon.

She was certainly tastier than her lamb roast.

Clausewitz evaded the grab made at him by Manfred and slid under the sofa. Manfred was late for his meeting in the kitchens across the way. Grabbing his talisman rabbit's foot for luck and his car keys, he was out the door.

FOOD FOR THOUGHT

"Mornin' boss," twanged the sub-cook.

They were a baggy-eyed group of late-rising wage-earners. It was tough going here in the former GDR with so few comfortable middle-class spenders. The restaurant in the Luisium landscape garden was in a financially precarious situation. Its innovative exclusion of smokers in a land of strong addiction was especially challenging.

Usually the culinary workers hung out in the courtyard clothed in cook's whites, the black buttons smart and double-rowed. There they slouched down, keen on inhaling. They drove little cars with windows perpetually open as wafts of stale air poured out. The hand not on the wheel curled around a red-ended ciggie.

Manfred Broadford, tall, dark-haired and athletic, did not smoke.

"Ladies and gentlemen," he began, "we are always on the frontier. Cooks have missions. Even in the most adverse of economic conditions we fight to win. Take our new barbeque titbit plate, piled with pork, steak and sausages. And to go with it we have simple pre-packaged, peeled and sliced potatoes. This means you just take them out of the plastic sack. Less work on the potatoes. More attention can be paid to the steak and pork. Remember to keep the heat sizzling hot. Scorch lines on the outside, blood red on the inside. What I want from you is attention to detail. Every action in a cook's sleight of hand counts!"

And he laughed a well-fed laugh.

He was being paid to teach them to squeeze money from the punters, so here it was: big white plates, the bigger the better. Then that inevitable salad out of a bag, leaves washed and picked by low-paid labour. Pork injected with water to make it weightier, and the chicken always cheap from the battery farm.

The one thing they couldn't cheapen was the sausages. People in Brandenburg, Saxony, Anhalt, and Thuringia knew sausages like connoisseurs did wine. Nuances of their centuries-old flavourings still tempted the palate. Surprisingly they hadn't rebelled against the truly awful taste of pre-sliced potatoes for roasting.

They simply never gave that crisp smart edge. Were his countrymen going to fall for ketchup or fries square like fingers?

None of this did he say aloud. Manfred was more subtle. His mind was like a cat's, oblique but effective. He would get them to behave. Cooks' tricks were a school unto itself. But that of course was not the end of it.

"Cooks are really like the secret service in white uniform," he thought. "What with smart black buttons, and very brawny too." He admired himself. He had buttoned up an exceptionally dazzling white jacket with Mao collar around his exceptionally muscular chest. His trademark black-and-white chequered handkerchief was tucked into his breast pocket. His black mane was coiffed back.

So he spoke to his rapt audience of underlings like a god. And they gazed up at him full of rapture.

COOK'S BROTH

The soggy sandwich dripped. Diluted mayonnaise spread like opaque Chinese white over the inadequate paper towel. Lettuce waved like green tongues between the wholegrain bread slices. Inspector Queberon's mouth had left a horseshoe hole where he tried to assuage his hunger.

Cluttered around the paper towel were plastic paperclips in lurid reds, greens and a sick yellow. Like confetti they had come to rest on reports and files. Inspector Queberon did not like working behind a computer screen. But paper reports marked with a post-it or page markers could become confused as well; the markers invariably fell off.

Hunting through his paperwork nonetheless appealed to him. It was analogous to his private treasury of accumulated knowledge. The piles of paper were to him what his brain was: a series of associations, the lateral-thinking brain as they used to call it. Often this turned up that odd and useful thought that floated up from unknown depths.

Today, everything snarled up in a traffic jam of half-pursued hunches. Didn't help that the report on Dr. Wilhelm Paternoster was as bland as the academic's personal details. The usual set of perfectly acceptable papers in history journals, themes topical and coinciding with the next necessary step on the career ladder.

It seemed he was totally transparent, a blameless denizen of the transition from former communist State to the capitalist version. No Stasi past, no membership in anything.

Just one incongruous find, a cookbook. Along with the usual wallet contents of a blameless man, as forensics undressed him they found in his pocket several sheets from what seemed like a proof for a book called *Salad Days*.

A whimsical title. Lettuce to Queberon was full of potential caterpillars. Paternoster's proofs contained handwritten corrections. Not in his miniscule copperplate ballpoint, however. The unidentified handwriting was lavish; the words scrawled with a fountain pen in blue-black ink. The nib must have been finely raked as the flourishes were almost calligraphic. Inspector

Queberon threw his soggy bacon and lettuce sandwich into the bin. *Salad Days* stared at him forlornly.

MANFRED SAT at his desk in majesty. His two screens were black without even a flicker. He had not gotten into the day's work. He stared in puzzlement at a hand-written manuscript composed in script he could not decipher. He presumed it was eighteenth-century hand-writing. It had come in the envelope that he was hoping would contain proofs of his new culinary bestseller, *Salad Days*.

The ink was faded and uneven. High loops gave the 'f' or the 'h' a distinctive otherness. These were, indeed, puzzling. The written word was almost an illegible scrawl.

ACADEMICS

Later, over a plate of excellent sauce hollandaise on freshly cooked asparagus tips and a glass of Saale-Unstrut, the dry and perfect accompaniment, a local culinary secret, Manfred relaxed. His next job was talking to a professor. If these were not female, they tended to be pushovers.

Career ladders were to men in academic fields like breathing apparatus to deep sea divers. Open up the climb and the feet stepped up on the rungs. Manfred's drooping cat's eyes glazed with happiness.

And here it was, the mouse itself. It was grey, naturally. And had a white shirt and tie with little insignias on it, like torches of learning. The nose was pointed, too. It sniffed.

"Professor Zaubertier, I presume?" Manfred didn't

have to greet him by citing Livingston in deepest Africa, since they had conversed previously, but decided this was just the thing for this occasion. Zaubertier was just too full of himself.

A young mouse, but already learning to sit up for titbits of the best Stilton going.

"Mr. Broadford? I am delighted to meet you again."

"Have a seat; and can I order you something? A beer perhaps?" Manfred thought beer and cheese and mice went well together.

"A coffee; black, please. I'm on my way to Berlin."

The usual put-down, thought Manfred. The professor was too busy to talk long with the manual classes. He'd make sure it was very strong coffee.

"Now if I can come to the point," said Zaubertier, "we are organising a conference right here in this place, in the courtyard, if the weather holds this year as it did last, with quite a few people from significant universities in Germany and abroad. Good food and drink is of the essence.

"You, if I may say so, have an unparalleled reputation as one of Germany's most innovative cooks. My research on the internet was exhaustive. Could we count on you to manage the culinary side?"

"No love but through the stomach," smiled Manfred.

The coffee was served and Zaubertier spluttered.

"That's the new manly brew for mid-morning. It

tests the testicles. Otherwise you'd better have a melange," said Manfred very, very seriously.

He waited until Zaubertier got the message.

"The usual mix of almost all male and a few token women academics?" he asked. "That's because I have to know volume. Men eat more and drink late. Universities are like the church no doubt; deacons will do, but no women bishops."

Manfred loved to bait anything as outwardly docile as Zaubertier.

ZAUBERTIER DEPARTED QUICKLY. His stomach felt tossed in Force Six caffeine. God, the new generation of cooks! Barely younger than himself and he in his forties. No one deferential anymore to the trained mind.

But food made a difference to conferences. He recalled a meal at University College London in their new dining room. It had been ultramodern in décor with what he privately called the blood and slash school of abstract art on the walls. A green putrid protuberance of scalpel-applied oils collided with a vertical spine of reds. It did not have a frame and it deserved none and dizzied his eyes as conversation faltered.

"Academia is strapped for funds these days," he had said to his neighbour in these surroundings a short time ago.

"Or has no taste buds," the female professor from America had said, "try abstracting the food you eat."

So, Zaubertier hunched out of the Orangerie with his wide mouth in a frown, still thinking of his coffee.

It was a glorious day in which he neither saw the nuthatches with their face paint—an inquisitive dash of black over their eyes—finding luscious insects in the crevasses of hundred-year-old oak tree bark, nor did he notice the whipped-cream clouds extravagant over the marzipan white sunlit summer leaves; in fact, he was the most unfeeling historian to ever walk in the subtle undulations of the Luisium landscape garden.

His mind was on university politics. His career chances lay with the perfect organisation of an international conference to which the big boys were coming. He was not a fool, for his PhD dissertation had been on networks of power in the early Enlightenment.

Athena's owl looked down on this human wisp of a man who walked aslant down the path. He came to a halt suddenly. The neat owl fluffed its patterned feathers. They fell softly into place. Then it closed its eyes against the too bright daylight.

"A goddamned faun!" exclaimed Zaubertier. He had come to a white-painted bridge with a gate and turned left, looking around to get his bearings. He came face to face with a white statue.

The tender lines of the white-faced faun with vine

leaves and grapes crowning his head looked away from him, lost in some exquisite dream. The hooves of his goat-skinned ancestors draped his shoulders. He seemed to think he was in his element, the Weymouth pines whispery behind him and the curve of sunlit water below. He did not move.

"There's no God," muttered Zaubertier to himself, gluing his gaze to the gravel path, "let alone those pesky pagan inventions. Apollo be damned. Or is it Minerva? Why did the bloody eighteenth century put pagan gods and temples in their gardens? Another bucolic idol, like the melancholic cow, Louise, that lived here; very hermaphrodite, to coin a joke, Hermes meets Aphrodite, ha-ha," Zaubertier muttered to himself, gluing his gaze to the gravel path. He did not look up again until he reached his car.

The Faun was related to the nature god Pan, and he whispered to the trees that Zaubertier was an unbelieving atheist.

HAVING FINALLY CAUGHT up with his aunt, Hugh leaned over the long oak table in the Eyserbeck House cradling his tea. His aunt's books were stacked willy-nilly like unlit thought-chimneys around him. She was sitting opposite, yet far away. He could tell by her brown eyes focussing on some far horizon line that she was elsewhere. Hugh was now sure she had recovered.

"That statue of the faun near the old dam who looks sideways eternally—either at the upsurge of water in spring or its drying in summer—that is the nature of water and woods. The statue, so exquisite in white, is the spirit that comes to you as you visit waterfalls or glens.

"But I must add," she whispered gently, "it's an effeminate faun so tender in its feelings for the ephemeral but recurring seasons. It embodies the return of hopeful spring leaves after the dying autumnal ones each year. I look into his marble eyes and believe there is hope in nature.

"I refuse to believe in death without resurrection every time I see the faun's gentle face. Pan guards the soul of every fleeting stalk of dried grass.

"And I am going to be on the heap they burn this fall, if I go to that conference," she concluded.

Hugh sighed. "You don't play according to the rules, aunt." He went on, in a chiding manner, his aunt the only woman he knew who could untangle his metaphor-laden speech. "Your goat-like nature makes you climb the rocky paths and should you chance upon vegetable patches you eat them unchecked.

"The wayward thoughts you have disturb those that like their facts stacked up like a hamburger. Nourishing mince-meat must be an oxymoron. Anyway, I like oxymorons. They should have plurals, there are so many of them being eaten!"

She turned to the window where outside the cherry tree waved its slant-eyed leaves in the stream of summer's mild breezes. She was certainly not going to inhibit Hugh.

She suddenly focussed on an event outside her window. She watched a cook in his white and black uniform. Then she saw a tall, black-haired male uncoil from one of the seats at the table in the corner of the courtyard where the cooks congregated. The antithesis of a faun.

SENTIMENTALITY

The conference *Thinking the Enlightenment* was held late that summer in the Orangerie and the courtyard of the stables that adjoined the Eyserbeck House. The chief cook Manfred, the tall, black-haired cook Zaubertier had engaged, made sure bellies were filled with good wine and nibbles and at a groaning buffet table.

Elizabeth's talk had divided the conference. She had earned the disdain of Wilhelm Zaubertier, there was no mistaking it. She saw part of the audience shake their heads.

She had tried to justify both Louise's and Henriette's miscarriage in terms of old-style women's marriage rites. They had been true to their vows, but their bodies had rebelled and shown how troubled they were.

The crux of the matter was that the miscarriages, the pregnancies that had gone wrong, had been the cause to both women of mental and physical pain. Both had suffered and this had triggered the friendship toward each other that had endured. This was the new closeness women now articulated when they shared intimately what bothered them.

Their husbands did not show the prolonged attention needed in such sorrow. The brooding over lack, over a child who was simply no longer there, not to be, was a sentiment best told and retold to those of the same sex.

In a detrimental fashion, often the whole genre of Sentimentality was laid at woman's door. Used thus, it could convict them as fools. They could be seen as useless, jabbering collections of self-pity.

Yet Elizabeth Hammerstein saw something different. She knew steadfast sorority was being built. Bridges of friendship constructed to last were being erected, no matter the burden put upon them. Stone upon stone, heavy and solid, was lifted into an arch. The bridges between women, weeping or coping with their loss, lasted. Women built their special female communities.

Elizabeth pointed out that Louise and Henriette had common ground. Their ties were primarily emotional, although the rationality of their situation played its part. In this, their feelings for one another, they knew exactly how physical pain became enveloping for both body and soul. They became one with the missing. In commiseration with each other, they could understand.

Sentimentality, Elizabeth said, was crucial to the bonding of Louise and Henriette and so many of the women of the time. It was important to acknowledge this factor.

Sentiment was close to compassion, but sprang from a need for women to communicate with women. It was empathy. There was bonding and commiseration, but above all, there was this emptiness with which women could emphasize—come to see their own bodily fate. It was one of the most crucial bonds. Louise and Henriette were forever close because they experienced one another's hopes, and then in hopelessness saw the love needed in this, each woman's plight. Their partners either divorced them or left them.

Elizabeth insisted on the value of feelings.

Only men—for the most part—turned a blind eye. And travelled another route. They wanted nothing better than to rationalize the pain and sorrow.

The intangible idea was that only at this point did Louise and Henriette realize what was at stake. It was emancipation at great risk, but they both managed it. It was insight. Neither would subject themselves again to be merely the carrier of what dynasty expected.

Elizabeth drew out the false security a pregnancy

brought with it that in essence was not to be; she foresaw how in sudden realisation both women knew they were independent entities, not merely the object of desire. It was a womanly insight not many cared to acknowledge.

From then on, Louise and Henriette shared values they prized. They themselves determined what mattered, far beyond the idea that women were merely valuable in marriage. They became themselves and dove into their fate.

LOUISE AND HENRIETTE

"Looking back at their lives you can see what happened after miscarriages and their failed marriages," said Elizabeth. She was catching up with Eva Delamotte, who in a moment of identification with the many plights of women had offered her red, pink, and white roses.

The archivist said, "You were quite radical trying to rehabilitate Louise. She is disparaged locally as a hypochondriac and ill-fitting wife of Vater Franz, the Prince. You'll be the centre of some horrid gossip!"

"Louise left all behind and tried to immerse herself in the ancients' cultivation of ideals and matrons, but independent ones. This comes out in her diary," countered Elizabeth, tired but satisfied after her talk. They were both having tea and Eva had sympathized with Elizabeth.

"Henriette took another path. She dispensed with the trappings of aristocracy. She became a teacher of young women."

"I know," said Eva. "I've studied the papers. Henriette took the obvious path open to her. She had Pietist leanings. The Pietists advocated a separation of the sexes except in marriage. This was not a culture of catering to wishes for representative progeny, but marriage based on equality: whosoever could help the other for the good of the community."

"I think we're singing from the same hymn sheet—as the Pietists would have it," laughed Elizabeth. It seemed to her she was making friends at last—and ones she cared about—ones that carried the wisdom of the past into the present. She wanted to intertwine Henriette with the women of today. She and Eva were inching forward.

"Henriette never married again after her divorce. Her life was given over to instruction to the woefully ignorant second sex of her times. She practised her duties to the end. It was her choice and therefore a statement of what she wanted."

This delving into a new and perfectly legitimate fulfilment had earned Elizabeth the nodding of female heads. Henriette's dedication was heroic in her time.

Louise was the more flamboyant of the two. She took supposed lovers, but left them. In all the hypochondria assigned her, she came out as her own woman.

"I really wanted to do no more than establish this. And yet criticism abounded. I championed the Unseen, a variant despised of material culture. This is not fact upon fact—this is a feeling, an emotion-based choice in the very restricted past, acting out what is possible—in the hope that women will choose independent routes." Elizabeth wavered, trying to be understood by Eva, but not certain now.

Elizabeth's early conjecture of womanly emancipation had merited only a shrug from Zaubertier, who had led the questions that made her admit she was leaping in the dark, bringing to light what may be hidden, that her conclusions may be supposition.

But Elizabeth was sure she had divined the buried treasure of female lives, and was proud to have dealt with what at first seemed invisible.

She wanted to justify the appearance of the ghosts everyone was hunting in history. But she wanted to give them separate rights.

In a moment of uncertainty, she shivered. Eva said kindly, "we have shared a lot; now we share the future."

CASTLE ON THE ELBE

H ugh let his pedals drift. He relaxed. Sitting on a bicycle was easy even with his still sore leg. At a certain speed bicycles coasted forwards by themselves. But this was only possible on well-maintained paths. He liked this one; smooth as an apple peel. The only drawback was aesthetic. The track was monotonous. Six kilometres straight ahead. Not bad for coasting though, he mused.

Helen had proposed this outing a few days ago. She wanted to show him the Elbe and the town Coswig just beyond the famous Woerlitz gardens. Most visitors confined themselves to sight-seeing on and within the sinuous dyke that embraced Woerlitz and the sightlines tucked within the landscape garden. But here was the real thing, the wetlands of the mighty river. Summer clouds combed the wide curves of pure nature.

Helen watched the darting swallows careening after insects. She too loved the motion possible on bicycles, not as slow as walking and not as fast as driving in a car. Minute things mattered: like this small infinity of cool morning in the middle of which was freshness itself.

Hugh and she had skated down the dyke beyond the gothic houses on the rim of the Woerlitz Park. The thin cut of the track to Coswig was first through meadows and then rimmed with trees.

They liked the same things. The awful gondola accident—that near drowning—had brought them ever closer.

Helen pedalled fast to catch up with the coasting Hugh. He was entering the long straight stretch that framed the spire of the church on the other side of the river on which lay Coswig.

Then the woodland closed around them once more. The very opposite of the gay, seemingly playful landscape enveloped them. Dense greens hide things, thought Helen. She coasted close to Hugh. Her feelings for this Celtic stranger were still a puzzle. But she felt drawn to him.

They rode side by side, watching the spire appear and disappear like a mysterious finger pointing at them. It gained height as they closed in on the vanishing point of the old straight track. They pedalled faster between water-hungry poplars. They became children, speeding ahead, competing, whooping challenges as they caught up, then sped past. Progress is easy on the straight and narrow.

Slightly winded, Helen braked. The bend in the road to the hotel by the ferry station was not far off. Hugh braked, too, and glanced back. She was standing there startled, vulnerable and pretty. He felt a tenderness he had not felt before. It was as if he would miss something that he had not known was precious to him.

"I thought I heard a clap of thunder," she shouted in his direction. And then she realized what the present sighing noise indicated. She added in a vexed tone, "my bicycle tyre is flat. It exploded."

She spotted a shard of glass. It lay sparkling innocently on the tarmac. Small woes are sent to try us.

Hugh picked up the glass and dropped it in the special bag he carried to keep rubbish in. He inspected the tyre which looked very flat. He pushed the bicycle forward and it bumped limply. Helen, watching, burst out laughing.

"You look for the life of you like you will implode."

"I don't like walking," said Hugh, quite grumpy.

"Just put one foot in front of the other," said Helen. And quite unexpectedly she leaned over and gave him a peck on the cheek.

Hugh stopped. He let the bicycle fall on the tarmac. He gathered her in his arms. The other bicycle went clunk too.

The approaching gaggle of tourists on their long-range touring bikes wavered but rebalanced as they swerved onto the cobbles of the old road that carried motorized traffic. It is the gift of the elderly to take all in their stride.

The men with their baseball caps sat straight even as cobbles bounced them sideways. Their wives in vivid blue windbreakers took it in their stride. One of the men shouted out: "was there an accident?"

"Hormonal thunderstorm, more like," his wife shouted back.

The avenue of trees remained unmoved, as always, by human emotion.

EVA DELAMOTTE SAT on one of the rickety chairs by a rickety table on the fairly empty terrace by the banks of the Elbe and in front of the hotel built there. She saw some elderly bicyclists dismount and lock up their touring bikes. They seemed the epitome of respectable middle age. Only those ridiculous baseball caps seemed out of place.

Whatever happened to nice straw hats with black bands? But they would blow off and roll away in the wind, thought Eva. She had fully recovered and was back in business as head of the archive.

She had made friends with Elizabeth. In her own way—neatly dressed, full of the authority of head archivist, reticent but firm—she was happy to support that 1960s initiative 'women's studies'. She was becoming radical—but showed her beliefs only discreetly.

She took a sip of her gin and tonic. She stretched her slim legs out, lazy and content to have found this hidey-hole. She had momentarily given up on the comfortable seats in the Tante Ju bar.

The river moved implacably northwards towards Hamburg. Thank heaven, Eva thought, for remoteness. No noise except for the burble of talk and the clink of beer glasses or the grunt of a dog or two shifting its weight under a table.

The passenger ferry on the Elbe was mid-stream. Eva watched it slide like a metal shovel in the current. To the north rose that old war horse of a castle in Coswig. It had once been an archive and depository of historical material. The ceiling in some of the rooms was now bifurcated by a vicious steel beam that frayed the wattle and daub. Ancient oak beams still sat cross-wise to the steel. Below, box upon box of archival deposits had run the length of the room.

The ferry was docking. Its steel lip-edge grated on

the cobbles that ended in river water. People got off, waved farewell to the ferryman. Simple people, ordinary people.

The castle sat inscrutable. At present an art consortium was refurbishing it. They were changing its box-like shape by dismantling modern additions. It would lose its oppressive boxed shape. Which was linked, Eva recalled, to its worst years. Coswig Castle had been a prison. In its vaults and ice-cold rooms political opponents of Fascism had sickened and died.

Eva had once been inside. She and the group she was with had vanished in long corridors and its tulip towers. The castle was massive. There was an extraordinary emptiness. It was as if all was hollow and history had gushed through the building in flash floods. There were many unexplored cells.

Never mind, Eva thought. She was here to plan. She had proposed this forgotten place on the banks of the Elbe for the next meeting of archivists from all over Germany. The view was romantic and the Elbe Terrace Hotel just the right size for a smaller group of scholars. They would fit in well here, so out-of-the way and yet oozing history. Although it was wicked to include the evil side of history as well as its enlightened passages. But after all, the castle symbolized both good and bad.

Eva wanted her archivists to produce cogent answers to various inquiries. The bevy of archivists was dutiful—

they wanted to illuminate and enlighten the public. Eva was adamant she could help. She wanted to listen and learn. It would be so different from Zaubertier.

The waiter advanced with another cup of coffee. Eva had her notebook opened on the table, wanting to write down what she needed to do. A list is best, she knew. But boring. It made her glance up.

Two familiar figures hove into view. They were pretty as a picture together.

FERRY RIDE

The blank windows of Coswig Castle looked out over the mighty windings of the Elbe. Only the very foolish would ever swim these waters. The swift current quickened circles that sped like manacles on the surface. They would twist under the watery surface anyone who fell in and drown them.

All castles look small from a distance. Two thick towers rose on each side of the terrace, unflinching and watchful, defining this one. The slender tower of the inner courtyard enclosed a winding stair. It wound and wound upwards in stone to the arcaded cupola upon which was placed a golden weathervane now rattling in the wind. The cavernous cellar rooms were too many to count and the clammy first floors were gutted. Iron bars covered the windows. The rooms were still subdivided into even more numerous cells and the doors had the strength of prison walls. Peepholes and locks were still in place. The mute stones exuded the sour breath of cruelty.

Romance is a trick of the light. The history that plays around the mighty walls of the past comes alive by how the sunlight vanishes and the sombre parade of clouds dims, sparkles, and shines, and imagined ogres stare inward from empty windows. Tricks of the light made the bulwarks and the massive towers leer.

Elizabeth was travelling toward Coswig Castle on the ferry. It had docked just below the Elbe Terrace Hotel. She stood transfixed by the castle looming over the running grey current of the river and becoming ever larger. The ferry was cutting the muscling water like a meat cleaver. The power of the current pushed the ferry across; it had no motor, only a steel cable slipping along one fastened across the river. Elizabeth was with a group from the conference that was going to tour Coswig and its castle. It was an excursion to mark the end of the conference. Afterwards all of those involved would depart.

She was uneasy because she saw not far away the wavy locks of Direktor Eszett. He was in his usual tweeds. He had chaired part of the conference.

"A curious custom," thought Elizabeth, "some German men favour the mimicking of the English. But they lack the English love for dishevelled casualness. The wavy locks of Direktor Eszett are battened down. No charming wind ruffles them." Then she added, betraying her judgement of him, "The hair oil is evident."

Elizabeth detected a certain rank smell, perhaps of tweed not laundered enough. Or was it her extreme dislike of an overbearing male? The smell of animosity?

On ferries no-one can escape those one does not care to meet. His eyes met hers and turned away as the ferry bumped on the concrete slipway. It had arrived at Coswig. The passengers moved as one to step onto the pebbled path that led up the bank. In their milling about Elizabeth was jostled towards the rear. She bumped into the tweedy Eszett.

Eszett had wanted 'Vater Franz', the Prince, to be feted as an Enlightenment hero. Instead the journalists of the *Mitteldeutsche Zeitung* had chosen Elizabeth as an historian who exploded the myth of dainty, insubstantial women. They liked the idea of feminism as a modern idea.

But Eszett now had a different motive. He wanted above all to know what Elizabeth knew about Henriette's last will and testament. He had been told, by one of his many informants, that Elizabeth had read the diary entries of Henriette. She might even know about Henriette's legacy and how it affected Babylonia's inheritance.

Eszett needed to keep Elizabeth very quiet—perhaps eliminate her entirely. He favoured the plans of Babylonia von Morizburg; and above all he desired Babylonia. But he did not want this linked in any way to himself or the landscape garden.

He was the first to speak. Elizabeth was staring at the water. The ferry was now unloading its passengers on the other side of the Elbe River.

"Such ineptitude. These ferryman can't even land properly or depart effectively. But this is a life-time sinecure. Keeps the unemployment figures down. Professor Hammerstein, I hope you are enjoying your brief stay with us?"

She looked into his unpleasant blue eyes. They were unreadable. They would remain blank until he saw his advantage. A mind preoccupied until, like a shark, prey is scented. A shark's eye is blank. Only blood focuses his reflexes.

Why do I feel threatened? Elizabeth thought; but out loud she said: "This is true summer weather to relish here, squalls and then lots of sunshine. I like sitting under green leaves which flicker in the sun. So different from never-ending rain. I live in the land of the rain gods talking."

Too fanciful, she thought, he'll think I'm just plain idiotic. Why does this man make me flip into nonsense?"

"Professor, I did not know you had such a poetic

soul. I thought the British possessed nothing but good common sense. They write such sound books, biographies without the metaphysics, books on philosophy without abstractions; they are such a formidable race..." He let the thought slide, looked vaguely into space.

Probably looking hard for someone else to talk to, thought Elizabeth.

"Everyone is individual; I just like clouds and blue skies," she lied. Not much conversation in that direction, she hoped. Maybe he would leave her alone.

"Ah. The painter Constable," he lisped. Again that crooking back of the flowing, oiled hair, that pride in his own profile. Showing off.

"The river and the grey green willows; the church spires, true," she answered. The ball was in his court.

The white teeth grinned at her, flashed. "Just so," he said.

"But let me ask you something else," he continued, "do you find our Louise pathetic and as ill as they make out? Those poor women had so little power; perhaps it was this simpering that drove the Prince away, aided and abetted by that strange woman from Lippe-Weissenfels, Henriette, Louise's sister-in-law. Middle aged and finished, both of them. Are you exploring our archives?" He emphasized what was surely contrary to everything she had said in her talk.

The shark wants blood, Elizabeth thought. "Henriette wasn't so very dull," she said. "She had money of her own and of course she disposed of her properties in her last will and testament. They might have an influence in the present day, especially on property values."

This was bait. Elizabeth wanted to see if he was interested.

"There are papers; they were formerly lodged here in Coswig," he said, "when the castle was used as an archive. But they were moved with all the many cardboard boxes of files. Sometime during the Second World War. And the indexes got confused. Henriette's will was supposedly lost," he added, trying to ascertain what she knew.

She looked at him carefully.

They were moving on the edge of the group near where the ferry docked. In the distance water meadows beckoned. The poplars marked the riverbank. These rose in mighty plumes of unruly leaves chattering in the wind.

The woman with blonde hair and well-cut trousers just ahead of me is going to turn around, thought Elizabeth. She will surely flirt with Eszett.

And indeed she did. The woman said in a gushing, playful voice: "*Herr Doktor* I just so adore that shop in the Woerlitz gardens by the restaurant, all those useful address books and napkins with garden motifs. How thoughtful that the Preservation Society would cater to our frivolous needs. So good of you to condone it. I go there frequently."

She was well-preserved and athletic. Her shirt collar was crisp, everything ironed. The trousers too had been ironed and on her wrists silver and gold bracelets jangled. Picture-perfect hair bobbed at mid-length.

Elizabeth was always hard pressed to find a redeeming feature in such constructions of the feminine.

But Eszett thrived on adulation. "The services we provide always augment our mission to reach out to everyone. Our gardens are justly famous because we serve the public. How kind of you to mention how much you like the shops. Have you travelled here from far away?"

Just as well, Elizabeth thought. I can ease away and escape this.

The ferry landed with a great grinding noise. People behind Elizabeth were jostling to take the path onwards. They were heading up the path to Coswig.

She saw ahead of her an old bastion enclosed by fishermen's cottages. This was the castle. The footpath, then an alleyway led up to it. The women and men from the conference trailed singly and in groups along the path. Many had now opened umbrellas. These toddled uneasily in the wind that arose with the drizzle. In a short time they would be gathering in a circle to hear a brief lecture on Coswig history by an attendant guide.

The umbrellas spread out, a vivid trail of red and orange and black and so many other colours. The myriad umbrellas and, below them, the people, gathered together whenever the guide made a short speech. The umbrellas, and the people, stopped before the renaissance portal, obviously meant to repel invaders. Undaunted, the circling umbrellas, and the people, filed through.

The inner courtyard was vast and studded with weeds and uneven flagstones. They were grimy with the debris of builders; almost slimy. Everywhere there were piles and obstructing heaps of brick and stone. Elizabeth took care to walk without slipping.

The tour guide was setting up his next explanatory session. Everyone closed around him. Elizabeth caught the last words.

"The castle is being renovated to become a centre for the visual and performing arts. A monumental task," he joked. "I will take you through a small room in which we have put up panels to explain the future envisioned for Coswig and then take you through the castle itself.

"Be very careful as we go inside; there is a lot of rubble. The rooms in the cellar have not been altered from the time when the castle was a prison. They still have locks and heavy doors. The corridors are clogged with demolished beams and walls. Debris is everywhere. If we lose you," he joked again, "you'll join the rubble and become tomorrow's exhibit of old bones discovered by enterprising archaeologists.

"I do sincerely warn you if you do not keep close to me as a group we may never find you!"

The umbrellas clicked shut. The group descended like a swarm of gnats. The buzz of footsteps reverberated from the low vaulting from which, to the right, the cell doors of the prison stood half-open. The locks were in good nick on the doors. Light filtered dimly through high windows divided by corroding iron bars. The air was dank.

Elizabeth tarried; she did not want to catch up with the more closely-knit crowd ahead. At its rear she could see Eszett unduly attentive to the white-shirted blonde.

At least the white shirt shows up in the gloom, Elizabeth pondered. Even though she had put her raincoat on, she felt chilled to the bone. Her vivid imagination grappled with the castle's sordid history. She stood by the door of the cell just next to her. She examined the double strength of its iron locks. Then she scrutinized the cell around the corner, out of sight of the close knit group around the guide.

Disturbed by shoes crunching grit and dust she watched Eszett detach himself and come toward her. People were concentrating on the uneven floor as they moved away towards to the stairs and into a shaft of light.

Eszett was leaving them behind and coming in her direction. No-one was in sight anymore except Eszett and Elizabeth.

Elizabeth felt tired. She did not want to be questioned about Henriette or her archival knowledge. She stepped into the cubicle of the cell that was around the corner with its heavy door. She did not want to be asked more questions. She hoped Eszett was leaving. That he usually just stayed long enough at conferences to be polite.

But she was wrong. Eszett had seen his chance. His objective was malicious. He suddenly, before she could protest, shoved her into the cell. Then he shut the heavy iron door. And he locked it quickly and firmly. He had gloves on.

The silence was that of centuries. She was imprisoned and left to die. No-one would look for her here. She heard his footsteps rush away. Shouting was useless.

No panic would register. There was no-one here. Only stillness.

There was no-one here that would notice. She repeated this to herself. The sensory chill indicated that here the state of things was immutable: walls and iron bars that stay in place forever. That no matter how much you move, you cannot move.

She suspected it was because she knew about Henriette; that she championed both her and Louise. If Eszett wanted her silenced this would look like an accident. He had simply taken advantage. He had quickly shut heavy iron doors and quickly locked them. The grating of the keys would not be remarkable on a site where moving bricks and cement by shovel was usual. As far as he was concerned, she was disposed of—everyone would think she had left early and was enjoying a coffee somewhere.

CAPTIVE

The walls were of uneven rock. The more Elizabeth looked the more they jutted out. It was as if they had developed teeth. They were black and grey. Some had a green sheen all over. She was the only breathing, warm thing incorporated here. And this was only the beginning of her nightmare.

It was cold beyond belief. Again the stones seemed to inch much closer. It was a tomb. The inescapability suggested burial. Eszett had known what he was doing when he had so effectively and finally shut the cell door. She had been tricked.

"I should have stood my ground, come what may," Elizabeth muttered, "not avoided Eszett. I promise—to myself I promise—even if this darkness proves final—to find more kindness and support—for all—yes all—in trouble..." and her voice petered out.

She was trying not to be frightened. She sat down huddled, her knees up to her chin. The cold crept under her coat. It was as if hands extended from those menacing stones and they gripped her mind. They wanted her hysterical. One part of her, the major part, wanted to give in to these hysterics.

She wanted to scream, to be delivered to warm arms. But then she realized the only human party, the sight-seeing party, had moved on. There was no one to hear her; no one to deliver her from cold and death. She was alone.

In her huddled and silent state she was alone. She saw no pathway to light. She saw only the enveloping dark. To her it was utter annihilation. There were too many things left unsaid.

"I did want friendship as a good both for myself and others—this was the beginning of the road to signal this —it goes beyond building careers..." There were tears forming.

How she longed not to drown in this darkness.

Elizabeth Hammerstein huddled her legs beneath her, stuffing her coat end as much as possible below her body, between her cooling body and the rocks. She wanted to avoid the walls of her prison. The ice-cold air of every winter since they were built inhabited the stones. And they had lain bare for centuries.

"This is what it is like in every prison," she thought. "This is entrenchment of fear and isolation. To be frozen to death is, really, an impartial object of the stone walls that enclose. How can I escape?"

She would become numb. She would lose all feeling.

Elizabeth was not above panic. In the creeping coldness in this godforsaken castle she lost all sense of time. She no longer knew what hour passed. In the eternal darkness she was a timeless skeleton. She got up, walked, huddled on the rocks once more.

She dreamed she was writing on a swaying bridge spanning an abyss. Her handwriting was wavering, but then she caught the words she needed.

"Every woman's life is a fairy tale written by destiny." She hoped this dreaming until the end would help her. But there was no bottom to the abyss. The ropes that kept this passageway over rocky valleys intact would fray.

In her dream some smart-ass academic was taking out his jack-knife. He cut the ropes. She flew into the abyss. There was a terrible darkness at the bottom.

Suddenly she stopped dreaming. Pain shot up her leg. It was a cramp. It shot up like fire. Maybe she should rise, flap all her limbs, be bird-like in death.

Her audience had loved ghosts as visions of the past.

But what of the present? Elizabeth noticed shadows. They flitted. They lightened the darkness and lightened the abyss. Watching this, Elizabeth became aware, slowly, of direction. The shadows rose and were pointing towards the thick, iron, window grate. This formed a series of bars intersecting. The iron bars were across the only window in the room.

Spectres come like bread to hungry lips. Shapes stood in the room with gestures to intimate something. But what? Elizabeth was going under.

SHE BATTLED the image of slithering inevitably down mortared stone into a blackness that would engulf her mind. She was a woman who lived by her brain. She resisted as well as she could the fall into the abyss of mindlessness.

At first there seemed no way out. She drew all her clothes more tightly around her. "Hug yourself, Elizabeth," she murmured quietly. "It matters not that you live.

"But it matters to not give in. The life I live may be a cauldron of chance, but it has one sure flame, the legacy of rebellion, feminine and the intellectual." Elizabeth felt an ember of anger. She fed the flames.

She did not know it, but the flickering shadows were really Louise and Henriette, come silently to see how she was faring. It took them some time to assume a more colourful shape. But right now they were hoping very much to witness Elizabeth getting angry. This would warm her up considerably.

At first she froze. Her voice caught. She stood stock-still. Her memories ran and ran down long corridors where there was no light.

But the ghosts' wonderful heads with nicely combed hair and their fashionable robes of white gauze swam in the dungeon's gloom. They flamed crimson and blue like pointers in the waning light on the watery walls. Elizabeth thought she was hallucinating.

And finally her rage caught fire. She spun from her rigidity into a phantom dance of heaving feet and drumming rhythms. She was no more that cool woman of intelligence. She was the fiend.

She was the bear. She was every looming shape in turn. She shouted words against the walls. Up past the bars. She rose tall and taller and took up the room and each phantom slid small against the slimy cage. She became a flame.

She groped for her talisman. The silver fearlessness of true worth gave her sustenance. She clasped a shape of heartwood. She had taken this found piece of wood to keep as she cycled through the bowing forest in Dessau-Woerlitz.

Elizabeth finally fell down in a heap. She had danced

her way to exhaustion—in defiance. Her heart was beating fast. She willed her body to get up again. Her clothes were smeared with sweat. The coat was rent by her colliding with the walls.

Was it her innermost wish to be saved?

Louise and Henriette became visible. They silently pointed their fingers at the iron bars. And in her exhaustion Elizabeth slowly realized that the bars were only leaning. They had been pushed into the stones to resemble prison incarceration—but they could be loosened. They could be wrenched from the smooth stones. The window could be opened.

Elizabeth crept upward, levering her feet stone by stone, rock by rock jutting out at her.

She reached for the bars. She could, did, draw them away from the opening.

She could crawl through the now bar-less window of freedom.

AND AT THE same time whistled notes skimmed in and out. A well-known melody took hold. Who could whistle a tune so well? She knew the notes and the melody. They brought back the joys of her Scottish home. Melody brought back memory.

This was a happy song. It was about mountains and thyme: those rolling hills in August covered in the purpling hazes of flowering heather and the smell of herbs scrabbling among the low bowing heaths of it. Summer is optimism.

It must be Hugh. Only Hugh would seek her. He must know she was missing.

But then the ballad stopped. She heard nothing.

She stood, feet apart. And then she too whistled, imagining the fragrant hills and the lochs below. The tune was the same she had listened to: it was there in the room, echoing. Elizabeth in exhilaration reached for the loose iron bars. She began to squeeze through the walls.

She whistled and drummed. She remembered the words. She sang the song. 'The Wild Mountain Thyme'.

She heard the window clatter open. And Hugh was honing in on noise and song. She cried tears but she was also stronger. She had confronted not only death, but herself.

WANTING TO KNOW

Hugh thumped his way up the double staircase that at its top housed Direktor Eszett's office, near the pinnacle meeting Eszett coming down the stairs.

"And who are you?"

Hugh's Scottish hackles rose. He countered by looking Eszett straight in the eyes and saying blithely: "I don't hold with superiority. You are mere flotsam and jetsam to me."

Eszett drew himself up and turned away.

Hugh spat the words 'Elizabeth' and 'death' at him. He had the satisfaction of seeing Eszett flinch before passing on his way as if Hugh were not there at all.

. . .

Eszett reappeared mid-morning. He was on his way to meet Babylonia von Moritzburg. He had chosen to have coffee with her at the Hotel Fuerst Leopold and bring her around to his way of thinking. And she would be all fresh and enticing. So stuff these Celts and their suspicions. He, such a superior being, would never be caught.

Babylonia was already seated at the bar. Turning towards him was a piece of her best flesh, her snow-white breasts, she purposefully unbuttoned her blouse just enough and her bra pushed her assets upward and forward. She obviously meant business.

"A lovely morning it is," said Eszett. "I've come to discuss the building of the luxury hotel you wanted overlooking our grumpy Vesuvius and all the scrappy, rain-dodging plants they put up there to thrive."

"Do clean it up." She smiled lasciviously. "I have the papers all ready. The ground of what is usually a turnip field belongs to me. I want turrets and the Gothic style —but high, something like The Shard in London. And lots of pools and seating. Rooms with sliding doors and balconies. I'm glad you are willing to envision sacrificing vegetation on Vesuvius, that hump of a replica volcano. But I hope you light it occasionally! Naturally, I'll advertise the Preservation Society's support."

"You know me—always interested in income! Dedicate a portion of the profit to the garden kingdom, and that's fine by me. But let us get on to better things. Let me take you to Berlin, where we can celebrate in style. Let me take you to the new Hotel de Rome." He gracefully lifted her hand to his mouth and kissed it.

ELIZABETH WAS prone under the sheets. She missed Hugh, but was too sleepy to register where he had gone. She wanted to send him to Eva to check the files.

These could reveal why Paternoster was killed and expose motives of who was behind it all. She had her suspicions, but she lacked evidence. A saying came to mind. Be aware of small things, like worms, that eat into great oak trees.

She called Helen, having failed to get hold of Hugh.

But all Helen could divulge was that Hugh was nowhere to be found. She suggested Inspector Queberon would certainly find him, if Elizabeth was worried.

The Inspector was not available either. This was because he was about to survey the abode of Manfred Broadford. He had a warrant.

To his chagrin, the cats got in his way. Old Fritz was stuck on the highest shelf and swishing his tail. Clausewitz was meowing and eyeing his counterpart, his competition, Fritz. The Inspector was just within the door of the flat that had been purchased from the Preservation Society. He was trying the door—which was open because of the cats—and he was looking inside.

Things were spick and span. In all there was little paperwork and that visible at a glance. He had come in vain. Then Old Fritz dished out a page with his furious tail. Clausewitz caught it in his paws. Clausewitz wanted to play.

The Inspector flew forwards. It was not a copy of *Salad Days*, but a script with 'f' and 'h' in funny collusion. It was the original of Henriette's will. And Old Fritz was swishing his tail out over its next page, adding insult to injury.

The Inspector looked down, taking the sheets from the aggressive Clausewitz and the cat gratuitously added a few bloody scratches to the Inspector's hands.

Indeed it was the original of Henriette's last will and testament. She had gifted the property adjacent to the Vesuvius to her lineage. It had jumped several aristocrats to land in the gift of Babylonia von Moritzburg.

The Inspector didn't bat an eye. But he gathered the evidence and was now more than certain that the head cook was involved.

Speculation had it that Manfred was allied to Babylonia. But there had been little outward show of this. The Inspector ruffled his forehead. The cats enjoyed his brief inertia. Old Fritz danced to the top of his head and earned a vicious slap. Clausewitz clawed at his booted feet. They were a team turning against him and they showed it.

Inspector Queberon was inwardly convinced that Elizabeth had been proven right. He finally could show everyone how it was done. Hans Homburg had met an accidental death as he tried to manoeuvre a gondola near the shore on the Woerlitz lake. He had died before a cocaine package addressed to Direktor Eszett could be hidden again. That was the white package that Elizabeth had seen. But it had gone down with the gondola.

The man who ran the drug trade for the pleasure of a select few was Manfred Broadford, who could collect money by way of tips and distribute by way of pastry delicacies. Manfred was enamoured of Babylonia—and she was baiting Eszett to get her the property and permission to build the luxury hotel.

Poor Paternoster had provided her with the necessary paperwork on this, her legacy. But he had been an irritant and potential blackmailer. She had gotten rid of him because she didn't like him and felt proud of it. Babylonia always conceived of herself as above the law.

"So far, so good," murmured the Inspector. "Now I'll just have to make the arrests!"

AUTOBAHN

Eszett wheeled his fast car out of the garage at Schloss Kuhnau. It was all arranged. He would meet Babylonia in Berlin. He had ordered a suite in the hotel with a huge and delicious bed. He would make sure it was classy and would impress. He revved his motorcar in happy anticipation.

What he did not know was the gathering of his ghostly opposition. Henriette and Louise had formed the team that was to pull him down. They disliked intensely his continual use of women as if they were objects of his own pleasure alone. Even worse was his desire to turn Woerlitz into a money-making themed parkland.

The vengeful ghosts of times past went to gather in the temple of Diana. This white house in the classical style was pitched on the dyke which was also the narrow road for bicycles that made for Woerlitz along the forest and dams of the Elbe River.

Louise von Anhalt-Dessau and Henriette looked into each other's soulful eyes. They were clothed in eighteenth-century garb, each with a gown that touched her feet and a white veil that framed the face.

Not far from where they gathered the screeching volume of high speed traffic resounded. The Autobahn with its immaculate tarmac spanned the mighty Elbe just beyond where Diana was honoured with her Temple. The white Temple was tiny compared to the lanes of modern speeding. Munich could be reached in five hours. Berlin in much, so much, less. The bridge over the Elbe was like a pair of suspenders clipped taut on an old mafia man; it was tense, dark-coloured, pinging with testosterone. The goddess Diana would have aimed her virgin arrows at its vibrations.

Louise and Henriette joined hands. They moved as one, their delicate gowns entwining. In ghostly reverie they swayed towards the Autobahn. They apprehended the swift gallop of Eszett's silvery projectile. It was diving in and out of the fast lane and leaping towards the gradient onto the Autobahn; it did not allow for any diminution of speed. The horn blew. The car was king of the road. Eszett was one with his vehicle, he gloried in his command.

He was driving fast on the Autobahn. The car careened in and out of the relatively slow lorries with their speed limitations. He was about to round yet another lorry as something strange got in his way. He saw it as a veil of white and a double silky presence. Eszett could not believe the figures: to him it was impossible that the woman, Louise, that he disparaged, and the Pietist divorcee, her friend, had blocked his fast getaway to Berlin.

He particularly objected to the sad, soulful eyes of Louise von Anhalt-Dessau. Her look was one of pity yet scorn. Eszett swerved. He careened towards the nearest lorry.

This was full of newly harvested nuts from Hungary. He burst its tailgate. Instantly he and the Autobahn were inundated with ripening nuts still in their hard green shell.

The things rolled with great glee all over the solid, well-kept surface of the Autobahn and cracked open. The silvery shine of his car was smudged with blackish lines.

His vision was obscured. He only caught the mocking stare of Louise and the pious glance of Henriette, under which he surmised a triumphant glare. The moment was frantic, as he had disturbed the fat, placid lorry and, out of control, it went for him. It seemed a pouncing tiger.

. . .

THE AUTOBAHN WAS CLOSED in the direction of Berlin. Inspector Queberon was called. Yet again he donned his plain-clothes Burberry jacket. A miserable loss of life on the motorway. Some fool had steered his flashy car onto the tail end of a lorry and had doused the asphalt with sticky nut-flesh.

Inspector Queberon was surprised to discover the bashed form of Eszett. He was unsettled to see the unaltered face of the Direktor in all its disdainful, arched-eyebrow glory deathly pale before him. The arms were limp, extending from their expertly sewn elbow patches; they had only reluctantly let go the steering wheel.

Inspector Queberon didn't tarry. This was a straightforward case. He only wondered at the good quality of white veil that entwined with the very ordinary sticky nuts that had taken possession of the Autobahn. Next to the police they blocked the bridge that was like suspenders and drew a driver's quick gaze towards the curlicues of the current of the Elbe and the luminous Temple of Diana. The goddess Diana's Temple seemed closed and the bicyclists that usually crowded the dam absent.

ELIZABETH KICKED THE SHEETS BACK. She wasn't going to

tolerate any defeat whatsoever, despite her evil experience in Coswig Castle and her immense tiredness.

She got up and went to the windows of the Eyserbeck House, and, to her surprise, she spied Manfred. The windows were all in a row, facing the courtyard. From there it was easy to see what was going on. It was Elizabeth's habit to go and look out. She usually meditated on what she was going to write on that day.

Manfred was being trailed by very subdued cats. But what was more he was arm-in-arm with Babylonia. This was most unusual in Elizabeth's view. The two of them did not seem a pair, thought Elizabeth. She believed their being together rather strange—and yet they were in plain sight.

Babylonia was chatting away, and Elizabeth caught only "Eszett" and "no way". Elizabeth tarried behind the curtains. Actually she was not too far away to catch part of what they were saying. The windows were single glazed.

Next she saw Manfred stop short and ask Babylonia whatever became of Henriette's will. Babylonia put her index finger to her lips and pouted.

Manfred sported about, waving *Salad Days*. But he was dead serious about getting his information regarding the luxury hotel from Babylonia. She could see that and succumbed far too quickly to his inquiry.

She fiddled with her décolleté. "Manfred," she said in

a sidling voice, "come away with me and taste the life of the rich; you'll only cook if you want. The lands by the Vesuvius are mine and the luxury complex will see us twiddle our thumbs the rest of our salad days."

She knew she was tempting. She was sure he would give in.

"Let me see," said Manfred, intent on not only seeing, but on getting the papers. He was now fixed on his own deal with Eszett. This involved the compliance of the *Herr Direktor*. And it would—very conveniently—let him set up a new clientele in the new luxury hotel. He would be able to find a passage along the canals in the landscape gardens as well. This would add to the convenience of his networking. He imagined greater wealth.

He wanted his fingers on the throttle, just like on the speedboat. He had used that very efficiently against the gondola. A pity it had not drowned all those in it. Such a lark. He could have gotten rid of the lot. He had practiced repeatedly on how he could hole a gondola and how to apply just the right amount of power to reverse his speedboat and never anyone the wiser.

Never mind Babylonia's infatuation, he wanted proof of her legacy and he wanted to run his cocaine empire. The suspicions of people like Eva Delamotte didn't amount to anything. She had no concrete proof. Nor would she get any. He would make sure of that. Certainly he got some satisfaction that Delamotte and

Inspector Queberon tried to criminalize him. In his mind's eye they deserved to flounder.

As far as he was concerned they were like puppets gesturing in the dark.

He had been proud of his warning with his marzipan cake, teasing Inspector Queberon.

His iron arms reached out for Babylonia and he bent her backwards. She dropped her handbag. He held her tighter. He would kiss and vanquish her. He almost succeeded.

But Old Fritz landed with much relish on the exposed expanse of breast so well-tended by Babylonia. Clausewitz did not want to be excluded from the warmth and the rosy pillows of breasts. He followed suit. But there was no staying where the slopes were so good, so slanted, more eye-catching than snuggly. Besides, cats' claws were not comfortable.

Manfred snorted at the intrusion. He tightened his grip on Babylonia. The cats jumped away. Elizabeth averted her gaze, but at the same time became aware of Helen entering the courtyard, looking for Hugh most likely.

Manfred twisted to rid the two of them from the cats. But as he held onto Babylonia, the wrench in her position made her bend lower. And the gun slid out of her handbag.

Helen just stopped and stared.

Rounding the corner behind her, however, was another figure. It was the well-defined and positive persona of Inspector Queberon. He too wished to consult Elizabeth, but as the gun dropped to the ground, his attention fixed on it. He dove forwards to retrieve it.

Immediately it was apparent to him that this was the gun used to shoot Paternoster. The pistol was of the right calibre. The scent of smoke and gunpowder told of its recent employment. Queberon was vindicated. And he would have the proof.

Manfred was caught out. He turned around. He dropped Babylonia. He caught his cats and made an innocent face of it. "Not me, guv..." was his look, until he saw the gun. Then it dawned on him what Babylonia had done.

Both men lunged forwards, but Helen got there first. She left the gun to them, but confronted Babylonia, who blurted out that Paternoster was expendable. Babylonia was very sure of herself. She was above them all.

Inspector Queberon, having seen the gun, advanced and handcuffed her.

Then he advanced on Manfred Broadford. Manfred was making no defences. But Queberon was still interested in asking him about the speedboat and the trade in cocaine.

"Let's start with those wedges of potatoes packed so thickly," he said. "Just what did they really contain?"

Manfred blustered in his dark-haired and tall frame. Inspector Queberon delivered a long shot. "And those speedboats on the Woerlitz Lake, were they anything to do with you?" And Manfred tried to hide it.

"I'm arresting you on suspicion of attempted murder and drug trafficking," said Inspector Queberon. He was both relieved and frowning because he hoped his direct attack would bring about the confession he expected from the cook. In any event, Manfred was cornered. He could no longer bluster and pretend innocence.

Queberon turned towards Helen. "I think I saw Hugh quite desolate and wandering among the reeds in old Prince Albert's domain. He is grimly meditating while he tramps about in the old vineyard on the lake there. When I caught a glimpse of him he seemed a bit grumpy and purple in the face."

Helen was torn between seeing to Hugh and witnessing this sudden arrest of Babylonia and Manfred. But she decided where her priorities lay and departed.

That left Elizabeth, who had advanced from behind her curtain into the morning sunshine. She witnessed how the accused admitted criminality. She stood in amazement, only just realizing how close to her abode the drug trade had flourished.

Her work complete both in her successful lecture and in her satisfaction with Inspector Queberon's arrests, she contemplated her return to the Isle of Mull.

Although, she thought, seeing the friends she had made, she might stay a little longer. She wanted to continue her work and have it matter for women's lives. But she wanted, also, to share and to be with her new friends.

And now, too, she was satisfied in seeing culprits made to pay for thinking only of how to indulge themselves. Also, she liked this landscape garden, and was pleased to see it remain true to its inspiring history, able to tell its original story.

EVIDENCE

Elizabeth Hammerstein happily engaged the people she felt accepted her champions, Louise and Henriette, for their embracing what even now is so important: friendship.

She had earned among others the respect of the archivist, Eva Delamotte. "Since seeing you defend these early forms of independence among women, I'll seek out an equitable balance! History is contemporary as well as delving into the past. It's as contemporary as they come," said the ever dapper Eva.

The archivist knew what disheartening trials Elizabeth had gone through. But she emphasized the future. "Gone are the dark days—the encroaching, bleak prisons—let's speak out for change!"

And her blue eyes twinkled.

Elizabeth was invited to eat cake with that accomplished librarian, Emma Specht. She tasted with pleasure the Sacher Torte she was handed. The trauma of ghosts and police had played itself out. She had written her book on Louise von Anhalt-Dessau and Henriette von Lippe-Weissenfels as ladies aware of their emancipation but also saddened by the false pregnancies connected to spouses fulfilling the wishes of a dynasty.

Emma Specht was as calm as her cake, happy with the thick, dark, chocolate and a touch of apricot jam. And so was Elizabeth. The filling under the tasty chocolate coating was from a jar of special jam that only Mrs. Specht could make. The cake was sheer perfection.

Elizabeth and Emma Specht were discussing the lot of Eva Delamotte. She had contacted Inspector Queberon about Manfred Broadford, having noticed a shard of the speedboat that had attacked them. The attack by the well-handled speedboat had made the gondola roll sideways and then sunk it and them. But a tiny shard of wood, painted with the speedboat's colours, had lodged in the gondola's side.

Eva had found the splinter imbedded in the gondola wreck when it was pulled out. She had seen this incriminating evidence when she had reimbursed the boatman for the loan of the gondola and paid for its subsequent restitution.

She had spotted the speedboat itself lying to dry on

its carrier off a hotel on the other side of the Elbe. She had asked who owned it. And trained as a minutely observant archivist, she had compared the boat with the splinter and then put it into a plastic bag and gave it to Inspector Queberon. It was what he needed. The evidence was building up nicely.

Queberon made a case for knowing all about the speedboat and the birthday cake to Manfred while the cook was being interrogated at police headquarters. Manfred dropped his pretence of innocence. He confessed.

Eva had been to see the Inspector numerous times. She had become used to his ways and his English eating habits. She had to admit she liked what she saw.

He just gazed intently into her eyes.

For Queberon this seemed more than admitting to passion. He ate an extra steak.

Hugh and Helen? They set off on bicycles and were forever happy. Sometimes they even forgot everyone else.

And there was even a twinkle in Elizabeth's eye. For here in this landscape garden she was happy at last, having gained friends and allies. Not all of them living.

Leasowes from the North

A NOTE FROM THE AUTHOR

After an academic career, creative fiction began late in life, but reflects my urge to lift knowledge gained about past events and people to imaginative heights. Themes can be elaborated, given crucial extensions, even humorous episodes, while still retaining real landscapes and places.

Writing helped to surmount my disability after my stroke that happened soon after my retirement. And all my writing is meant to challenge, but also to bring enjoyment.

If you've enjoyed reading this book, please look out for the rest of the series to see what else life has in store for Elizabeth Hammerstein and Inspector Queberon. Please also spread the word with a review on Amazon, Goodreads, Waterstones, Kobo or any other suitable forum. These are immensely helpful.

You can keep up to date with my writing, and see some of my artwork inspired by the landscape gardens that feature in my novels at sibylpress.com.

ACKNOWLEDGMENTS

A huge Thank You to Jim Paterson, my husband, for both the mundane tasks that are so challenging in everyday work when caring for the disabled and the intellectual talent he has that helped me a great deal when publishing this book. And importantly I owe much gratitude to Claire Wingfield for her undaunted courage in paying attention to every detail in reading this book from start to finish. She also helped edit this book and did more than anyone in accepting both the humour and the seriousness of characters and setting. I also want to thank especially Martine and Frank Kreissler and the many archivists in Dessau that helped in my academic work and interests at the time.

Lightning Source UK Ltd.
Milton Keynes UK
UKHW011553260422
402078UK00004B/235

9 781838 042004

GLORY DAZED

CAT JONES

Glory Dazed was first performed as part of the
Old Vic New Voices Edinburgh Season 2012
at the Underbelly, Edinburgh, on 2 August 2012.

GLORY DAZED

CAT JONES

CAST

in order of appearance

Carla	**Chloe Massey**
Leanne	**Kristin Atherton**
Simon	**Adam Foster**
Ray	**Samuel Edward-Cook**

CREATIVE TEAM

Director	**Elle While**
Producer	**Fliss Buckles**
Designer	**Becky Warnock**
Fight Director	**Rachel Bown-Williams**
Music	**Scott Goodison**
	2 Billion Beats
Set Design	**Peter McNally**

The Company

Cat Jones (Writer)
Cat Jones is the founder and Artistic Director of Second Shot Productions, a film and theatre production company based within HMP & YOI Doncaster that employs serving prisoners and ex-offenders. She was recently awarded a Butler Trust Award by HRH Princess Royal for her work in prisons.

Cat's first play *Rendered* was runner-up in the Theatre503/Old Vic New Voices Award. In 2011 Cat won the BBC Alfred Bradley Bursary for radio drama for *Glory Dazed*. The play was produced at the 2012 Edinburgh Festival Fringe in partnership with Old Vic New Voices where it was awarded the Holden Street Theatres' Award that saw it transfer to the 2013 Adelaide Fringe. It will also tour to Soho Theatre in 2013. Other theatre includes: *Shorty* (National Youth Theatre); *The Natives* (Old Vic New Voices 24 Hour Plays).

Cat has been part of the Royal Court's advanced studio group and Channel 4's 4Screenwriting programme. She is currently commissioned by Radio 4 and the Manchester Royal Exchange where she is Pearson Playwright in Residence.

Elle While (Director)
Elle's directing credits include: *Kingstonia* (Kingston Rose Theatre/Bad Physics); *Knock Knock* (The Roundhouse); *That Face* (Bristol Old Vic Theatre School); *Country Music* (West Yorkshire Playhouse); *The Great Switcheroo, I see myself as a bit of an Indiana Jones figure* and *Making Babies* (Theatre503); *The Jewelled Sea* (The Lowry); *Short Chalk* (Shared Experience Youth Theatre); *Street Kids* (Bolton Racial Equality Council). Numerous productions whilst employed as Youth Theatre Director at the Octagon Theatre, Bolton, including: *Mad World, Millboys, Blackwood, The Magic Finger* and *Just So Stories*.

Associate/Assistant Directing credits include: *The Winter's Tale, The Taming of the Shrew* (RSC); *The Sunshine Boys* (The Savoy, West End); *Hamlet* (Young Vic); *Cause Célèbre* (Old Vic); *Eden End* (ETT); *Onassis* (Novello, West End); *Rum and Coca Cola* – UK tour (Talawa and ETT); *Death of a Salesman* and *Cinderella* (West Yorkshire Playhouse); *The Caucasian Chalk Circle* (Shared Experience, West Yorkshire Playhouse and Nottingham Playhouse); *Anthropology* and *Pitching In* (Latitude Festival).

Fliss Buckles (Producer)

Fliss works for Second Shot Productions as a Producer/Director, having helped set up Second Shot as the first prison-based social enterprise in the country to offer its serving prisoner employees the opportunity to study the Level 3 BTEC in Creative Media Production. Fliss completed her MA in Film Studies at Exeter in 2011, receiving a Distinction for her dissertation film *Back on Road*, a short that explores the release process at HMP & YOI Doncaster through the eyes of three prisoners as they prepare for release and the impact the system has upon their lives. *Back on Road* won Best Documentary at the Exeter University Film Awards 2012 and was shortlisted in the Soho Short and Aesthetica Film Festivals 2012. Fliss is currently working on her first fiction short for production in 2013.

Becky Warnock (Designer)

Becky has a background in design and fine art, but went on to train at the Central School of Speech and Drama in Applied Theatre. Since graduating in 2010, she has specialised in running applied arts projects with vulnerable community groups, particularly prisoners, ex-offenders and refugees. She now works as Creative Arts Manager at Only Connect, a creative arts company in King's Cross, but also as a freelance photographer, artist, film-maker and designer.

Kristin Atherton (*Leanne*)

Kristin trained at LAMDA. Her theatre credits include: *Mansfield Park* (Theatre Royal Bury St Edmunds); *Brontë, Mary Shelley* (Shared Experience); *The Importance of Being Earnest* (English Theatre of Vienna); *Bee Stings* (Theatre503); *Confessions of a City* and *An Enemy of the People* (Sheffield Crucible); *Tale of Two Dogs* (Out of Order Theatre); *The Devil You Know: Lost Soul Music* (Pleasance Islington); *Harold Pinter: A Celebration* (National Theatre); *Iphigenia* and *Much Ado About Nothing* (Sheffield Crucible). Film and television include: *Absent* (dreamthinkspeak) and *Out and About* (Granada). Radio includes: *I Love You S.W* (BBC) and *The Fearless Youth* (Roundhouse Radio).

Samuel Edward-Cook (*Ray*)
Sam trained at RADA. His credits include Walter Storey in *Land Girls 3* (BBC) and *Magwitch* in Viola Film's prequel to the Dickens' classic, *Great Expectations*. The film had its London premiere in May 2012 and has now begun its festival tour including Cannes Film Festival, Montreal and Mexico. Theatre credits include Mack in *Boys* by Ella Hickson, directed by Robert Icke (Headlong). Sam has recently finished filming with Cillian Murphy and Sam Neil for the BBC's new epic gangster thriller *Peaky Blinders*, which is due to air in autumn 2013. Sam's credits whilst at RADA include: Heracles in *Heracles* (directed by Seb Harcombe), John Proctor in *The Crucible* (directed by Toby Frow), The Waster in *Ladybird* (directed by Seb Harcombe), Dada in *Our Lady of Sligo* (directed by Jonathan Moore), Bill in *Small Craft Warnings* (directed by Alex Clifton), Banquo in *Macbeth* (directed by Nona Shepphard).

Adam Foster (*Simon*)
Adam trained at Mountview Academy of Theatre Arts. His theatre credits include: *Hamlet* (Sheffield Crucible); *Crying in the Chapel* (Contact, Manchester); *Bay* (Young Vic); *The History Boys* (National Theatre UK tour and West End); *Twelfth Night* (Donmar West End); *Dead Fish* (Crucible Studio/Reform Theatre and UK tour); *Revolution* (Old Vic New Voices 24 Hour Plays); *Julius Caesar* (Leptis Magna Theatre, Libya); *God's Official* (Reform Theatre UK tour); *Gutted* (Angelica/Tristan Bates); *The Puzzle Women* (Dead Earnest/Sheffield Theatres). Television includes: *Prisoners' Wives* (BBC/Tiger Aspect); *Emmerdale* (ITV/Granada); *Doctors*, *Paradox* (BBC); *Coronation Street* (ITV). Film includes: *Pusher* (Vertigo Films). Radio includes: *Call the Doctor* (BBC).

Chloe Massey (*Carla*)
Chloe read English at Cambridge and trained as an actor at LAMDA. Her theatre credits include: *The 24 Hour Plays* (Old Vic); *Bush Bounce* (Bush); *Dream Plays* (Traverse); *Calm Down Dear* (Pleasance Islington); and *Hometown Glory* (Manchester Royal Exchange). Film includes: *Want of A Wife: A Foreplay* (directed by Justin Hardy) and *Dig* (directed by Duncan Pickstock). She is also a playwright and the artistic director of the Darkbloom Theatre Company.

Special thanks to:
Old Vic New Voices, Soho Theatre, Holden Street Theatres, IdeasTap, Underbelly, Only Connect, HMP & YOI Doncaster, Nick Hern Books, Katie West, Ralph Dartford and Alex Brenner.

Second Shot Productions is a theatre and film company based within the walls of HMP & YOI Doncaster. We employ a combination of serving prisoners, ex-offenders and others to deliver a range of services from film-making and graphic design through to drama and arts projects in custodial and non-custodial settings.

Though we're a company and trade for profit, as a social enterprise, all of that profit is invested back into our projects. We're committed to providing education, training and employment to serving prisoners and ex-offenders and using the arts to facilitate positive change.

Second Shot Productions currently employs fifteen serving prisoners at HMP & YOI Doncaster who work for the company full time. They are trained to deliver our services whilst working towards a BTEC in Creative Media Production.

Glory Dazed is Second Shot's first full-scale professional theatre production. It was rehearsed at HMP & YOI Doncaster and prisoners and ex-offenders were engaged by the project as stage managers, set builders, graphic and web designers, photographers, film-makers and musicians.

Visit us: www.secondshot.org.uk
Email us: info@secondshot.org.uk
Follow us: @_SecondShot

**OLD VIC
NEW VOICES**

As important to us as what goes on stage is our award-winning programme Old Vic New Voices (OVNV), which nurtures talent, inspires young people and opens up our theatre to new and diverse audiences.

TALENT

Emerging theatre-makers are offered support for creative projects, ongoing professional development, and invaluable networking opportunities with peers and industry.

> *'It has done an incredible amount in terms of professional development both individually and as a company'* (Producer)

EDUCATION

Renowned projects that give schools access to free theatre tickets to every Old Vic production, as well as bespoke learning experiences at the theatre, in the classroom and online.

> *'It was great to have talented performers come to the school – a real inspiration'* (Teacher)

COMMUNITY

Creating innovative, ambitious productions that engage hundreds of people as performers, researchers and crew, all drawn from our local communities with ages ranging from 16 to 76.

> *'Life affirming and life changing'* (Performer)

Visit us: www.oldvicnewvoices.com
Email us: newvoices@oldvictheatre.com
Follow us: @oldvicnewvoices

www.sohotheatre.com

London's most vibrant venue for new writing, comedy and cabaret.

Bang in the creative heart of London, Soho Theatre is a major new-writing theatre and a writers' development organisation of national significance. With a programme spanning theatre, comedy, cabaret and writers' events and home to a lively bar, Soho Theatre is one of the most vibrant venues on London's cultural scene.

Soho Theatre owns its own central London venue housing the intimate 150-seat Soho Theatre, our 90-seat Soho Upstairs and our new 1950s New York meets Berliner cabaret space, Soho Downstairs. Under the joint leadership of Soho's Artistic Director Steve Marmion and Executive Director Mark Godfrey, Soho Theatre now welcomes over 150,000 people a year.

> 'Soho Theatre was buzzing, and there were queues all over the building as audiences waited to go into one or other of the venue's spaces. I spend far too much time in half-empty theatres to be cross at the sight of an audience, particularly one that is so young, exuberant and clearly anticipating a good time.' Lyn Gardner, *Guardian*

Soho Theatre Bar
Soho Theatre Bar is a vibrant, fun bar where artists and performers can regularly be seen pint in hand enjoying the company of friends and fans. Open from 9.30 a.m. until 1 a.m., with free Wi-Fi, serving breakfast, lunch and dinner, with a new, super-quick and tasty burger, bagel, pizza and salad menu, Soho Theatre Bar is the perfect place to meet, eat and drink before and after our shows.

Soho Theatre Online
Giving you the latest information and previews of upcoming shows, Soho Theatre can be found on Facebook, Twitter and YouTube as well as at sohotheatre.com.

Hiring the Theatre
An ideal venue for a variety of events, we have a range of spaces available for hire in the heart of the West End. Meetings, conferences, parties, civil ceremonies, rehearsed readings and showcases with support from our professional theatre team to assist in your event's success. For more information, please see our website sohotheatre.com/hires or to hire space at Soho Theatre, email hires@sohotheatre.com and to book an event in Soho Theatre Bar, email sohotheatrebar@sohotheatre.com.

Soho Theatre is supported by Arts Council England and Westminster City Council.

GLORY DAZED

Cat Jones

To Mum, there at every step.

Characters

RAY, *mid-twenties*
CARLA, *mid-twenties*
LEANNE, *late teens*
SIMON, *mid-twenties*

Author's Note

The following was written in response to a number of discussion groups and workshops attended by ex-servicemen who are serving prison sentences at HMP & YOI Doncaster.

They were asked for their thoughts on why ex-servicemen are over-represented in the prison population. The figure is disputed but some professionals put it as high as ten per cent.

Thanks to John Biggin, Debbie Hall, Fliss Buckles, Steve Winter, Jo Mackie, Julia Tyrrell, Leo Butler, Clare McQuillan, Matthew Booth, Erin Carter, Sue Roberts, Charlotte Riches, Jo Combes, Julie Gearey, Iona Vrolyk and to all the prisoners both ex-servicemen and otherwise who gave so generously.

C.J.

This text went to press before the end of rehearsals and so may differ slightly from the play as performed.

Lights up.

A tired backstreet pub in Doncaster, after hours. CARLA, LEANNE *and* SIMON *in silence as though frozen. They all stare in the direction of the door. It is a long time before anyone speaks.*

LEANNE. D'yer think he's –

CARLA/SIMON. Shhh!

LEANNE *(whispers)*. D'yer think he's gone?

CARLA *(whispers)*. Dunno.

 Silence.

RAY *(from outside the door)*. I know yer in there!

SIMON. That'd be a no then.

RAY *(banging on the door)*. Let me in!

CARLA. What we gonna do?

SIMON. I dunno.

RAY. Open the fuckin' door!

LEANNE. Ask him what he wants.

CARLA. We know what he wants.

LEANNE/SIMON. What?

CARLA *(realises she doesn't know)*. Go on ask him then.

SIMON *(to* LEANNE*)*. Go on.

 LEANNE *goes to the door.*

RAY *(banging)*. Let me in! Yer hear me? I'm not goin' nowhere.

LEANNE. What d'yer want?

RAY. To be let in.

LEANNE. Well, who is it?

RAY. Ray.

LEANNE. Ray who?

RAY. How many Rays d'yer know?

LEANNE (*thinks*). None.

RAY. Oh come on, Denise, open the door!

LEANNE. It ain't Denise.

RAY. What?

LEANNE. It ain't Denise.

RAY. Really?

LEANNE. No.

RAY. Well, go and get her then.

LEANNE. She ain't here.

RAY. Why not?

LEANNE. She left.

RAY. Yeah?

LEANNE. Yeah.

   Beat.

RAY. Get the sack, did she?

LEANNE. Nah, moved on to better things.

RAY. Really? Well, good for her.

LEANNE. Yeah.

SIMON (*whispers*). Get rid of him!

LEANNE. Well, I've got to go now. Bye.

RAY. Nah, don't go. Let me in.

LEANNE. I can't.

RAY. Why not?

LEANNE. Cos Simon –

   SIMON *silences her with a look.*

   – wouldn't like it.

RAY. What, is he there, is he?

SIMON *shakes his head frantically.*

LEANNE. No.

RAY. I bet he is. I bet he's right there shakin' his head and lookin' like a proper twat. Ain't yer, Simon?

RAY *bangs on the door repeatedly.*

SIMON (*whispers*). Tell him to shut the fuck up!

LEANNE. Shut the fuck up!

The banging stops.

RAY. Did yer just tell me to shut the fuck up?

LEANNE. Yeah. But only cos yer gonna wake up the whole street!

RAY. I'm gonna burn down the whole fuckin' street if yer don't let me in! D'yer hear that, Simon?

Beat.

Simon!

SIMON (*whispers*). We're gonna have to let him in.

CARLA. No!

SIMON (*whispers*). I don't want the police here.

CARLA. Please, Simon.

SIMON. And it's Ray. We can't just leave him on the doorstep.

CARLA. Why not?

SIMON. Go and wait in the toilets for a minute. I'll get rid.

LEANNE. D'yer know him then?

SIMON. Go on.

LEANNE. Who is he?

CARLA/SIMON. Shut up!

SIMON. C'mon, Carla, it'll take five minutes.

CARLA. Alright, but yer better be quick.

SIMON. I will be.

Exit CARLA.

Go on then, open it.

LEANNE *opens the door.*

Enter RAY. *He bursts in, agitated and sweaty. He has a big dash of blood down the front of his T-shirt.*

Evenin', Ray. Out for a little stroll, are yer?

RAY. 'Bout fuckin' time!

LEANNE. Jesus, look at the state of him. Is that your blood?

RAY. Yer really ain't Denise.

LEANNE. I'm her replacement.

SIMON. She only started last week. We have covered the basics of door-openin', but to be honest...

RAY *goes to the window and looks out.*

I've met gerbils who learn quicker.

LEANNE *glares at* SIMON.

RAY *closes the curtains.*

Yer ain't bringin' trouble here, are yer, Ray?

RAY. Course not.

SIMON. It's just I can't help noticin' that yer seem a bit out of sorts.

RAY. I'm alright.

SIMON. Been fightin', have yer, Ray?

RAY. Just a straightener.

SIMON. With who?

RAY. Some bloke.

SIMON. And is he alright, is he? This bloke. Does he think it were just a straightener?

RAY. Me wife here, is she?

SIMON. No.

RAY. Yer sure?

SIMON. Not unless she's hidin' in the toilets.

LEANNE *stares at* SIMON *in disbelief.*

RAY. She ain't at the house. I went there already.

SIMON. Yer sure yer okay, Ray?

RAY. Yeah. Why?

SIMON. Yer don't look okay.

RAY. I need to speak to Carla. Where is she?

SIMON. I dunno.

RAY (*to* LEANNE). Get us a drink, will yer?

LEANNE *looks at* SIMON *for permission.*

SIMON. We were just finishin' up, Ray. We don't really lock-in like we used to.

RAY. A vodka.

LEANNE *looks at* SIMON *for an answer.* SIMON *nods.*

LEANNE *goes behind the bar to get* RAY *a drink.* RAY *sits down.* LEANNE *brings the drink.* RAY *downs it.*

Same again.

SIMON. Yer sure that's a good idea?

RAY. I'm shakin'.

SIMON. I can see.

RAY. Every bit of me is shakin'. But it's okay.

SIMON. Really?

RAY. I'm runnin' out of time. But it's okay cos I know what I need to do.

SIMON. What's that then?

RAY. Yer get to see what's really important when yer've got no time left. It's so fuckin' clear it's unreal.

LEANNE. Are yer dyin'?

RAY. Only of bloody thirst. Where's that vodka?

LEANNE *goes to the bar.*

She must have taken the kids to her mum's. I'll have this then I'll go over there.

SIMON. It's very late to be callin' on an old woman. Yer'll scare her half to death.

RAY. Good. Old witch.

SIMON. Look, Ray, I'm the first who'd have her chucked in the Don. I'm just thinkin' of Carla, that's all.

LEANNE hands RAY his drink. He downs it and grimaces.

RAY. Jesus. Yer still waterin' down the spirits? (*To* LEANNE.) He does that, yer know? Two parts bloody water.

SIMON. I don't.

RAY. He does.

SIMON. Give over.

RAY. Admit it.

LEANNE. Do yer?

Pause.

SIMON. Yeah, a bit.

LEANNE. Yer tight git!

SIMON. It's not that. I just don't like drunk people.

LEANNE. Yer the boss of a pub!

RAY. He's a comedian is what he is!

SIMON. Actually I like to think of meself more as a superhero. Sober Man! Secretly savin' the pissheads of Doncaster from 'emselves.

RAY. We're unsavable, mate!

Pause.

Right, I gotta go.

SIMON. Wouldn't yer be better off waitin' till tomorrow?

RAY. For what?

SIMON. Goin' to see her mother. It's a full moon. She's prob'ly boilin' toads or somethin'.

RAY. Have yer not heard what I've just said? I'm seizin' the day.

SIMON. Well, can't yer seize tomorrow instead?

    RAY *stares at* SIMON, *bursts out laughing then grabs his face and kisses him.*

RAY. I love you, Simon. I'm not sure yer ain't a faggot but I love yer anyway.

SIMON. Thanks, Ray.

    RAY *gets out a mobile phone and searches for a number, still laughing to himself.*

RAY (*mimicking* SIMON). 'Can't yer seize tomorrow instead.' That's a classic that is.

    RAY *puts the phone to his ear.*

    A second later, a phone rings on the table that CARLA *was sitting at.* RAY*'s good mood vanishes. He glares at* SIMON *as he ends the call.*

SIMON. She didn't want a scene, that's all.

RAY (*shouts*). Carla, I know yer here! Carla!

SIMON. Yer need to go, Ray. There's no use speakin' to her when yer in a state.

RAY. Carla! Carla!

SIMON. Carla, he knows yer here.

    CARLA *appears from the ladies' toilets.*

RAY. Carla.

CARLA. What are yer doin' here, Ray?

RAY. I needed to see yer. Yer don't take me calls.

CARLA. Yer been fightin'?

RAY. I need to talk to yer, Carla, and I ain't got long.

CARLA. What's goin' on, Ray?

RAY. Can we go outside? It's private.

CARLA. Why ain't yer got long? Has somethin' happened?

RAY. Please, Carla.

SIMON. I think yer better off stayin' in here, Ray. I mean, if it can't wait till tomorrow.

RAY. Five minutes, that's all.

CARLA. I'm not sure it's a good idea.

RAY. We were married, Carla. And now yer can't give me five minutes?

CARLA. I can. Just not tonight. Not when yer in this state. Go home and get cleaned up. We'll talk tomorrow.

RAY. No. Why are yer all so fuckin' obsessed with tomorrow? It has to be now.

CARLA. But why, Ray?

RAY. Cos it does.

CARLA. Then say it if it's so important.

RAY. I can't. Not in front of everyone.

CARLA. Yer've had yer choices then.

Pause.

SIMON. Yer'd better go, Ray.

RAY. Had I, Simon? Had I better go? Don't sound right, that, without a big fella stood behind yer. (*To* LEANNE.) I used to be that big fella.

CARLA. Please, Ray.

RAY *notices the fruit machine.*

RAY (*to* SIMON). Got any coins for this?

SIMON. It's gettin' late, Ray. Almost two.

RAY. We used to stay up all night. Go straight for a fry-up in the mornin'. Remember?

SIMON. Yeah.

RAY. I'm starvin'. Do us a roll, Denise.

LEANNE. I'm Leanne.

RAY. And I'm Bobby fuckin' Sands, me.

LEANNE. Yer what?

RAY. Bobby Sands? Hunger striker? Never mind. Just do us a roll, will yer?

SIMON. Will yer go then, Ray? Once yer've eaten.

RAY. Course.

SIMON (*to* LEANNE). Get him ten ones. I'll do the roll.

RAY. Don't forget yer pinny.

Exit SIMON. LEANNE *goes to the till. She takes out some coins and brings them to* RAY.

RAY *puts the coins in the fruit machine and starts to play.*

So you're Denise's replacement, eh?

LEANNE. Yeah.

RAY. Upgrade I reckon. That girl had a face like a slapped arse and an arse like two Transits fightin' for a parkin' spot.

LEANNE. She's me cousin.

RAY. I were very fond of her. Taught me a lot about the world, as it happens.

LEANNE. Really, like what?

RAY. Like not all fat girls are bubbly.

LEANNE. Oi! She's not that fat!

RAY. Are you kiddin'? Last time she went sunbathin' on a beach, Greenpeace tried to put her back in the sea! She were an arsey mare and all, had a pout on her that could sour ale.

CARLA. I thought she were lovely.

RAY. Course yer did. Women like ugly women.

Beat.

Where's she gone then, Denise?

LEANNE. To have a baby.

RAY. Well, that explains the fat belly.

LEANNE. She's adoptin'.

RAY. Poor bastard.

LEANNE. Oi!

RAY. But enough about yer mardy-lardy cousin. What about you?

LEANNE. What about me?

RAY. Why ain't yer a stripper or somethin'?

CARLA. For God's sake, Ray.

RAY. Don't mind her. She don't like it when I speak to gorgeous women.

CARLA. Everyone just wants to go home, Ray. Yer stoppin' everyone gettin' to bed.

RAY (*to* LEANNE). Yer've got the arse to be a stripper, you.

LEANNE. How d'yer know I'm not? This could be me day job.

RAY. It's night-time.

LEANNE. Yer know what I mean.

RAY. I do as it happens. I've got a night-time day job too.

LEANNE. Really? What's that then?

RAY. Guess.

Pause.

LEANNE. I reckon yer a bouncer.

RAY. I reckon *you're* a right little bouncer and all, ain't yer?

LEANNE *giggles*.

CARLA. Yer pathetic, Ray. She's a little girl.

RAY. Not built like that she ain't.

LEANNE. Am I right then?

RAY. Yer are. Come here and collect yer prize.

RAY *puts his arm around* LEANNE*'s waist.*

LEANNE (*giggles*). Get off! Where d'yer work then? I might have seen yer.

Enter SIMON *with a plate of food. He sets it down beside* RAY.

RAY. Worked here for a bit. (*Gesturing towards* SIMON.) I were Delia Smith's bodyguard.

LEANNE. Yeah?

RAY. We had some nights in here, I can tell yer. I'd be over there drinkin' and I'd get a text from Simon behind the bar. 'Get yerself over here, it's kickin' off.' I'd come over and he'd have told some kid they're not gettin' served. Only they've taken one look at him and pissed 'emselves. Then I'd rock up behind 'em, 'Yer mother's just phoned, son, yer drinkin' chocolate's done, get yerself off home.' Nine times out of ten they went without a whimper.

Beat.

Remember that one time, Simon? Them teenage girls wouldn't leave.

LEANNE. What did yer do?

RAY. Slapped their arses for 'em.

LEANNE. Yeah?

RAY. Yeah.

CARLA. I heard yer sleepin' in a van.

SIMON. Carla!

RAY. Yer what?

CARLA. That's what I heard, Ray. That yer sleepin' in a van, takin' showers in the swimmin' baths.

RAY. That's bollocks, Carla.

CARLA. Just what I heard.

RAY. Well, yer'll get a bad belly, won't yer, swallowin' all that bullshit.

Pause.

(*To* LEANNE.) Yer want to see a photo of me doin' me proper job?

LEANNE. Go on then.

> RAY *leads* LEANNE *to the bar. He looks for something but doesn't find it.*

RAY. Simon, where's me photo gone?

SIMON. We had to take it down, Ray.

RAY (*to* CARLA). That you, was it?

CARLA. What?

RAY. Get him to do that, did yer?

CARLA. No.

RAY. Liar.

SIMON. Take it easy, Ray. It weren't her. It were the guy from the brewery.

RAY. What guy?

SIMON. Area Manager. Said it's a pub not a town hall. Said it were political. That it could offend people.

RAY. How can a picture of a British soldier offend people? We're in Britain, for fuck's sake.

SIMON. I think it were cos yer were wavin' a flag.

RAY. Wavin' a flag not an Afghan fuckin' baby.

> *Beat.*

A raghead was he? This manager?

LEANNE. Yer shouldn't talk like that.

RAY. Oh, let me guess. He's yer cousin too, is he? Yer from one hell of a family, you!

SIMON. He's a white guy, Ray. From Sheffield.

RAY. We must be the only country in the whole fuckin' world that's scared to wave its own flag. What a joke, eh?

> *Silence.*

LEANNE. So yer were a soldier then?

RAY. Yeah.

LEANNE. In Afghanistan?

RAY. And Iraq.

LEANNE. Did yer ever see a dead body?

RAY. Hundreds.

LEANNE. Did yer ever shoot anyone?

RAY. Yeah.

LEANNE. Really?

RAY. Right in their face.

SIMON. There's no need for that, Ray.

RAY. It's just the truth.

LEANNE. Me brother's thinkin' of joinin' the Army. I want him to.

RAY. Get him out of this shithole.

CARLA. So he can get shot at in other people's shitholes.

　　RAY *takes out a pack of cigarettes. He goes to light one.*

SIMON. Yer shouldn't really smoke in here, Ray.

　　RAY *lights the cigarette and takes a long drag on it.*

RAY. He'll never know friendship like it again. We had some laughs, I can tell yer. Dance of the flamin' arseholes. Fuckin' brilliant.

CARLA. Yeah cos yer've not really been mates with someone till yer've got drunk and set fire to their backside, have yer, Ray?

LEANNE. Yer set fire to someone's backside?

RAY. Course not.

　　Beat.

　　I set fire to bogroll shoved up someone's backside.

LEANNE. Oh.

RAY. Ended up walkin' like he'd been fingered by an elephant.

CARLA. Does he have a girlfriend, yer brother?

LEANNE. Yeah.

CARLA. Tell her to run a mile while she still has chance.

RAY. Ignore her. He'll see amazin' things. Get to go to places where yer can see the stars, without all the smoke and shit in the way. I've never seen the bear as clearly as from the desert.

LEANNE. Yer saw a bear in the desert?

RAY. Jesus Christ, yer not sharp, you, are yer?

SIMON. There weren't a bear in the desert, Leanne, it were in the sky. Made of stars.

LEANNE. Oh.

CARLA. I've always thought it were stupid that.

RAY. What?

CARLA. That thing about stars in different shapes. They don't look like any of the things they're meant to.

RAY. Course they do. Ain't yer seen on the telly when they draw the outline round it? It looks just like a fuckin' bear.

CARLA. Everythin' looks like a bear if yer draw a bear around it, though, don't it?

RAY. Don't mind me wife, she can be a right little vinegar-tits.

CARLA. That's *ex*-wife, Ray. Ex. It's only two letters but they're like bloody release papers to me.

Pause.

RAY. Yer wanna play a game, Leanne?

LEANNE. Dunno.

CARLA. No.

RAY. Don't listen to her. It's an Army game. Yer can tell yer lad about it.

SIMON. Have yer finished, Ray? It's prob'ly time we were closin' up if yer have.

RAY. I'm gonna let me food go down for a minute, if that's alright with you, Simon.

SIMON. Yeah, course.

RAY. Right, Leanne, the game has three rules, okay?

LEANNE. Okay.

RAY. The first rule is this. If yer think of the game, yer've lost the game. Right?

LEANNE. Right.

RAY. The second rule is –

LEANNE. Think of it how?

RAY. Just think of it. Like yer thinkin' of it now, ain't yer?

LEANNE. How do you know?

RAY. Well, cos yer talkin' about it, ain't yer?

LEANNE (*confused*). Yeah.

RAY. The second rule is that if yer lose the game, yer have to tell everyone yer've lost it, yeah?

LEANNE. Yeah.

RAY. And if yer lose it, yer have to down a shot, yeah?

LEANNE. I'm not very good with shots.

RAY. Yer better not lose then, had yer?

LEANNE. I'm not sure I want to play.

RAY. It's too late for that. The last rule is that no one can lose the game for two minutes after someone else has lost it. Got it?

LEANNE. I think so.

CARLA. Yer don't have to play his stupid game with him, Leanne. This is what he does.

RAY. Really? Is it what I do, Carla? Get people to have a laugh. I'm such a bastard!

Beat.

Where's Jamie and Warren, by the way?

SIMON. Food gone down, Ray?

CARLA. At me mum's.

RAY. While yer piss away the family allowance in here.

SIMON. Cos it's prob'ly time we all got off home.

CARLA. It never bothered yer when we were together.

RAY. Well, it bothers me now.

CARLA. Yeah cos you're Dad of the Year, ain't yer?

SIMON. Carla.

CARLA. He almost pulled Jamie's arm out of its socket last time he saw him.

RAY. Cos yer've turned him into a whingin' brat, Carla. Me dad would've beat me like a drum if I'd acted like he does. There's boys all over the world half his age fightin' wars and runnin' farms.

CARLA. Well, he ain't one of 'em, Ray.

LEANNE. I think he's a great kid.

RAY. Yeah well, opinions are like arseholes, ain't they, Leanne? Everyone's got one, don't mean I wanna hear about it.

LEANNE. That's charmin'.

CARLA. That's Ray for yer.

Pause.

RAY. I'm sorry. I'm only messin' with yer.

LEANNE. Well, I'm goin' if we're not gonna play yer game.

RAY. We are playin' it.

LEANNE. No, you two are fightin'.

RAY. That's the beauty of the game, yer can do both.

LEANNE. Well, that don't sound like much fun for the rest of us.

RAY. Who said anythin' about it bein' fun? It's meant to get yer pie-eyed. Talkin' of which, go and get yerself a shot.

LEANNE. Why?

RAY. Cos yer lost, didn't yer?

LEANNE. How?

RAY. Yer mentioned the game. Which means yer thought of the game.

LEANNE. What?

RAY. Get me a drink and all while yer there.

LEANNE *looks confused*.

Chop chop.

LEANNE, *still confused, goes to the bar.*

(*To* CARLA.) You're smilin'.

CARLA. What?

RAY. Yer were smilin' just then. Yer were thinkin' about us playin' the game, weren't yer?

CARLA. No.

RAY. Yes yer were. Yer were thinkin' about the night I taught it yer. It were here. You couldn't get yer head round it either.

LEANNE *arrives back with the shots*. RAY *downs his*.

(*To* LEANNE.) Down it then.

LEANNE *downs her vodka. She grimaces.* RAY *and* CARLA *laugh.*

Jesus Christ. Look at the face on it. Like Denise lickin' piss off a nettle. (*To* CARLA.) You made faces like that. Got so pissed yer could hardly walk.

CARLA *continues to laugh*. RAY *laughs along*. CARLA *and* SIMON *exchange glances*. RAY *notices*.

(*Still laughing*.) What?

RAY *stops laughing*.

What?

CARLA. I must've been a pretty good actress, that's all.

RAY. What yer talkin' about?

CARLA. That night. Every time yer went to the bar to get me a vodka, Simon were givin' yer a water instead.

RAY. No he weren't.

CARLA. He were. At one point, yer drank mine instead of yours and yer were so far gone yer never even noticed. Me and Simon were pissin' ourselves, weren't we, Simon?

SIMON. I can't really remember.

RAY. Yer sly bastards.

LEANNE. Couldn't yer of done that for me?

RAY. There's no honour in cheatin', Leanne.

CARLA. It's a game, Ray. It's meant to be a bit of fun. Only there's not much you couldn't take the fun out of, is there?

RAY. We're havin' fun, ain't we, Leanne? Go on, get yerself another one of them down yer.

LEANNE. I'll be sick.

RAY. No yer won't.

LEANNE. I'll not be able to walk home.

RAY. I'll look after yer.

LEANNE. I ain't lost the game.

RAY. Now yer have.

LEANNE. But Carla just said it.

RAY. Don't be a sore loser, Leanne.

   LEANNE *goes to the bar to get a drink*.

CARLA. Jesus, Ray, is this what it's come to? Force-feedin' drinks to teenage girls? Why don't yer go the whole hog and buy a trench coat.

RAY. That's very funny, that is.

CARLA. Is it?

   Pause.

RAY. I want to see me kids, Carla.

CARLA. Well, yer can't.

RAY. Why not?

CARLA. I told yer before. Yer sleep in a van, Ray. Yer shower at the swimmin' baths.

RAY. And I told yer that's shit.

CARLA. I don't believe yer.

RAY. So the boys'll spend the whole of tomorrow stuck indoors while you lie in yer fart-sack stinkin' of gin.

CARLA. I got 'em Nintendo Wii.

RAY. Nintendo fuckin' Wii!

CARLA. Yeah.

RAY. Well, that's alright then!

CARLA. Cost a fortune, Ray. Not that yer'd know much about the price of things.

RAY. I could take 'em out, Carla.

CARLA. Yer not the least bit interested in takin' 'em out and yer know it.

LEANNE. I thought Simon were takin' 'em to football anyway.

RAY. What?

SIMON. For fuck's sake, Leanne.

LEANNE. What? He's sayin' yer don't look after the boys when yer both brilliant with 'em.

RAY. Why is he takin' my kids to football?

SIMON. I don't have to if it's a problem, Ray.

CARLA. Yer don't have to answer to him, Simon.

RAY. Carla?

Pause.

CARLA. Me and Simon are goin' out.

SIMON. Oh Jesus.

RAY. Goin' out where?

CARLA. Goin' out, Ray. With each other. Boyfriend and girlfriend.

LEANNE. Oh, didn't he know?

SIMON. No, Leanne, he didn't know.

Pause.

RAY. Him?

CARLA. That's right.

Pause.

RAY. Him!

CARLA. Yes, Ray, him!

There is a long pause. It could go either way, but eventually RAY *bursts out laughing. He laughs for a long time before composing himself. The others watch on, bemused.*

RAY. I'm sorry, I shouldn't. It's just –

RAY *dissolves into laughter once more.*

Still laughing intermittently, RAY *goes behind the bar, helps himself to a bottle of vodka, brings it back to the table, pours himself a glass and drinks.*

CARLA. What's so funny, Ray?

RAY. Nothin'.

CARLA. Well, obviously somethin' is.

RAY. How hard up are yer, Carla? After everythin' yer've ever said about him.

CARLA. I've never said anythin' about him.

RAY. Only every time they showed a photofit on *Crimewatch* yer were like, 'That looks like Simon Braithwaite.'

CARLA. I never did.

RAY. Yer said he were a dead ringer for a paedophile. That he looked like a right wrong'un.

CARLA. Just ignore him, Simon.

RAY. Remember when we heard he'd signed up to that datin' site on the internet? I said he were so desperate he'd fuck a stab wound. Yer laughed yer arse off.

CARLA. He's talkin' shit.

RAY. Yer said, 'Jesus Christ, who would?' and it's fuckin' hysterical that the answer is you!

RAY *dissolves into laughter once more.*

And what happened to likin' stocky fellas, Carla? I've seen more meat on blokes on a cancer ward.

CARLA. Just go, will yer, Ray. Yer just tryin' to cause trouble.

RAY. I'm sorry. It's a shock, that's all. No hard feelings, look.

RAY *puts out his hand to* SIMON. SIMON *views it with suspicion.*

C'mon. I won't bite yer.

CARLA. Just leave it, will yer, Ray.

RAY. Leave what? I'm offerin' the hand of friendship here. Some blokes wouldn't be so easy-goin'. He is shaggin' me wife after all.

SIMON *goes to shake* RAY*'s hand.*

Boo!

SIMON *jumps.* RAY *puts his hand out again.*

I'm only messin' with yer.

SIMON *shakes* RAY*'s hand.* RAY *pulls him into a full embrace.*

Look at yer. Like a dog with two dicks. Let's have a drink, eh? (*To* LEANNE.) Grab a glass, Leanne. (*To* SIMON.) We can swap notes.

LEANNE *brings a glass to* SIMON. RAY *fills it.*

CARLA. Simon, what are yer doin'? I want him to go.

RAY. Get used to that, Simon, she always wants somethin'.

CARLA. Simon.

SIMON. It is gettin' late, Ray. I appreciate how yer bein' and that.

RAY. Then have a drink with me.

SIMON *and* CARLA *exchange glances. She implores him not to, but* SIMON *looks apologetic. He takes a drink.*

Well, me best mate and me wife together. I couldn't be happier.

SIMON. We never meant for it to happen, Ray.

RAY. Yeah? Then how come it did?

SIMON. I dunno. Carla stopped behind to help me clear tables one night.

CARLA. Only we never cleared tables, did we? Well, I mean, we cleared one but that were for –

SIMON. I don't think we need to get into that, Carla.

RAY. At least now I know why she don't take me calls.

CARLA. It ain't his fault. I've been tied up.

RAY. Tied up, eh? Didn't have yer down as a kinky one, Simon.

CARLA. Grow up, Ray.

RAY. Get used to that and all. She's no sense of humour.

CARLA. Cos life were a laugh a minute with you, Ray, weren't it?

RAY. Excitin' though, eh?

CARLA. Not really.

RAY. You think so, don't yer, Leanne? That voddy kickin' in yet?

LEANNE. Yeah it is. Don't think I can play any more.

RAY. Play what?

LEANNE. That game.

RAY. Drink!

LEANNE. No I –

RAY. Drink! Yer never ever stop playin' the game, Leanne. I've got a mate who calls me up out of the blue every so often just to tell me he's lost and he's downed a shot for it.

RAY *pours* LEANNE *a shot.*

There's a good girl.

LEANNE *downs the shot.*

SIMON. I think we've prob'ly all had enough now, Ray.

RAY. Off to bed then, are yer, Simon?

SIMON. Yeah, I expect so. I'm done in.

RAY. Off to bed with me wife?

Beat.

That sounds funny, don't it?

CARLA. Hysterical.

RAY. Off to bed to fuck me wife.

LEANNE (*laughs*). That sounds *really* funny.

CARLA. Just go, will yer, Ray?

RAY. Leanne don't want me to go, do yer, Leanne?

CARLA. Yeah, she does.

RAY. Leanne?

LEANNE. I dunno.

RAY. Well, would yer be havin' more fun or less fun if I weren't here?

LEANNE. Well, I'd prob'ly be takin' the bin bags out now so less fun.

RAY. There yer go then. Drinkin' with me is more fun than takin' the bins out. Yer heard it from the horse's mouth.

CARLA. Bins still need doin', Leanne.

RAY. Fancy yerself as the landlady, do yer, Carla? Got yer feet well under the table, ain't yer? Never saw yer settlin' for a barman though. Yer wanna borrow me uniform, Simon? She used to beg for it when I were in that.

SIMON. Yer alright.

CARLA. He don't need it, Ray.

SIMON. Carla.

RAY. Is that right?

CARLA. Yeah.

Pause.

In fact, why don't yer take the boys to football tomorrow, Ray? Simon and I could do with a lie-in.

CARLA *looks at* SIMON *suggestively.*

RAY (*laughs*). I wouldn't get too excited, Simon.

CARLA. Why's that, Ray?

RAY. Well, he prob'ly already knows that two kids down the line yer not much of a dick-grip. Little fella like him could get lost up there.

CARLA *throws a drink in* RAY*'s face.*

CARLA. You bastard!

LEANNE (*laughs*). Yer asked for that.

RAY. Shut yer mouth!

RAY *pushes* LEANNE, *by the face, backwards off her chair.*

CARLA. Ray!

SIMON. Leanne!

SIMON *helps* LEANNE *up.*

You okay?

RAY. She's fine.

SIMON. Fuckin' hell, Ray!

RAY. What?

SIMON. She's a girl.

RAY. And? What difference does that make? I've seen girls in headscarves with rifles. I didn't hold the fuckin' door open for them!

CARLA (*to* LEANNE). What d'yer think of him now, eh?

RAY. Oh, don't milk it, Carla!

RAY *walks away.* SIMON *and* CARLA *see to* LEANNE, *pouring her a drink, checking she's okay, etc.*

CARLA. Are yer alright? Sit down here. There we go.

SIMON. Are yer hurt?

CARLA. Course she's hurt, he sent her flyin'!

Meanwhile, RAY *strips off his wet T-shirt, revealing that the blood that was on it has gone through and stained his skin. He notices it and wipes at it with the T-shirt. Most of it comes off. He goes to the bar and helps himself to a bottle. He drinks straight from it then takes it over to the fruit machine and puts in a coin.*

Jesus, she's shakin'.

SIMON. I think it's more shock than anythin'.

CARLA. She's white as a sheet.

SIMON. Ray, I think yer better go.

CARLA. Is that it? He's just hit her.

RAY. He's a pussy, Carla. I could've told yer that. Anyway, I never hit her.

CARLA. Don't you talk to me.

RAY. Fine.

Silence other than the fruit machine.

The fruit machine jackpot pays out.

Unbelievable. One fuckin' coin!

RAY *scoops up the winnings and puts them in his pocket.* CARLA, SIMON *and* LEANNE *stare at him in disgust. He notices them.*

What?

CARLA. Is there somethin' wrong with you? Are yer actually tapped in the head?

RAY. I never hit her!

CARLA. Oh, shut up, Ray. No one wants to hear from yer. I've had enough of this, Simon, I'm goin'.

SIMON. Carla, wait!

RAY *blocks* CARLA*'s path.*

RAY. Don't go. I need to talk to yer.

CARLA *sidesteps* RAY.

CARLA. Fuck off!

SIMON. Carla!

CARLA. And you.

> CARLA *gets her things together.*

> RAY *goes to the bar and takes a key that is hanging on a hook on the wall. He goes to the door and locks it. He puts the key in his pocket. The others watch him.*

> What did yer just do, Ray?

> *Pause.*

> Ray?

RAY. This ain't how I wanted it to be, Carla.

CARLA. Are yer stoppin' us leavin' now, is that it?

RAY. I thought yer'd listen to me. I came here to tell yer somethin' important and I thought yer'd listen, stupid bastard that I am.

CARLA. Well, yer have a funny way of makin' people listen, don't yer?

RAY. Please, Carla.

CARLA. No.

RAY. Well, yer not goin' nowhere till yer do.

CARLA. Fine.

> CARLA *sits down.* RAY *sits down.*

> *Long silence.*

> SIMON *starts clearing the glasses away.*

> For cryin' out loud, Simon!

SIMON. What?

CARLA. Just leave it, will yer!

> SIMON *stops tidying.*

> *More silence.*

Go on then, Ray, I'm listenin'.

RAY *pours himself a drink. He drinks it.*

Well, go on.

Pause.

Ray!

RAY. I have to get out of Donny, Carla. Tonight.

CARLA. And?

RAY. And I want yer to come with me.

CARLA. Yer've got to be kiddin' me.

RAY. No.

CARLA. Why the hell would I do that?

RAY. Because yer love me.

CARLA. No, Ray, yer've got that confused. It's the opposite, in fact, I hate yer and if yer want to know why, just look at the state of her.

RAY. I'm sorry about that but yer shouldn't of chucked yer drink at me, Carla.

CARLA. Yer know what, I'm not doin' this. I'm goin' home.

CARLA *goes to leave.*

RAY. Sit down.

CARLA. No.

RAY. Sit down. I'm not gonna tell yer again.

CARLA *realises he is being serious and sits down.*

Pause.

CARLA. Why are yer makin' me stay here, Ray?

RAY. Because yer have no fuckin' right to hate me after everythin' we've been through.

CARLA. You have no fuckin' right to expect anythin' else!

RAY. We don't need to sort any of this out now. We just need to get the kids and get on the road.

SIMON. C'mon, Ray, yer havin' a laugh with us, ain't yer, mate?

RAY. No, Simon, I'm not, but yer know what is a good joke? You callin' me 'mate', yer thievin' lyin' bastard.

CARLA. Okay, Ray, let's drag the kids from their beds, stick 'em in the car that we don't own and get on the road. Where are we goin', by the way?

RAY. Brighton.

CARLA. Brighton.

RAY. Me mate's got a flat there but he's goin' on a tour. I thought we could take yer mum's car. Be there by the mornin'.

CARLA. This gets better. We're gonna steal me mum's car –

RAY. Borrow it.

CARLA. Sorry, we're gonna borrow me mum's car and we're gonna go to Brighton. And what exactly are we gonna do there, Ray?

RAY. Whatever yer want, Carla. Swim in the sea. Eat fish and chips. Walk on the pier. Whatever. It'll be like Skeggy last summer but all the time.

CARLA. No it won't, Ray, cos that were a holiday and what you're talkin' about is a life. Are yer thinkin' that we'll feed the boys Brighton rock for breakfast and candy floss for lunch and they can sell deckchairs on the beach instead of goin' to school?

RAY. We'll work it all out when we get there.

CARLA. Well, that is just brilliant. Even for you.

RAY. We ain't got time for yer to think about it, Carla.

CARLA. Trust me, Ray, I'm not.

RAY. I'm riskin' everythin' in bein' here. I'm runnin' out of time.

CARLA. Please unlock the door, Ray.

RAY. The police are lookin' for me.

CARLA. Well, we never worked that one out. We thought the T-shirt were a fashion statement. Lady Gaga or somethin'.

Pause.

Would I be right in sayin' that ain't your blood, Ray, and that yer've given some poor sod a designer face to go with *his* designer T-shirt?

RAY. Somethin' like that.

CARLA. And now we're supposed to be scared of yer, are we? So scared that we're just gonna let yer lock us in?

CARLA *looks at* SIMON.

Tell him how daft that is.

SIMON. It *is* daft, Ray.

RAY. Yeah?

RAY *stares at* SIMON, *then takes the key out of his pocket and places it on the bar.*

Then take it.

Everyone looks at SIMON. *He doesn't move.*

Go on.

SIMON. This is stupid, Ray.

RAY. Not really. If yer want the key, take it.

Pause.

LEANNE. Go on, Simon, take it.

Pause.

Well, if you won't I will.

LEANNE *makes a move towards the key.*

SIMON. For fuck's sake, Leanne, will yer shut up and sit down!

LEANNE. He can't just lock us in.

SIMON. Yer pissed, Leanne. Sit down. Now.

LEANNE *sits.*

RAY. Even a fish struggles in a net, yer pathetic piece of shit.

Silence.

CARLA. Did yer kill him?

Beat.

Ray?

RAY. Course not. But he's pretty bad.

Pause.

Felt his nose break. Felt his ribs crack.

CARLA. Jesus, Ray.

RAY. I can't go to prison, Carla.

CARLA. Then yer better get off to Brighton, hadn't yer?

RAY. Not without you.

CARLA. We're not even together. Why would yer think yer could walk in here and get me to go on the run with yer?

RAY. Cos we should be together, Carla. You, me and the boys. Everythin' else is bullshit.

CARLA *feels for something on her head. She finds it and offers it to* RAY *for him to touch.*

CARLA. Feel this.

RAY. No.

CARLA. D'yer know what it is?

RAY. Carla –

CARLA. Do yer?

RAY. Course I do.

Pause.

CARLA. Don't think yer meant it. Hemmed yer in, didn't I? The first time yer came home. Before I knew any better.

RAY. Carla.

CARLA. I were daft enough to think yer'd come back through that door the same bloke who went out.

RAY. I did.

CARLA. We had a lovely meal. Cooked it all from scratch. And it were perfect till about ten when yer said yer wanted to go out. I'm like, 'What a selfish prick, first weekend back and he wants to be out with the lads.' Course it were the beers yer were cravin' as much as the boys. If I'd had a fridge full yer prob'ly wouldn't of bothered.

RAY. I needed to get out.

CARLA. And I'm pullin' at yer clothes like a stupid little girl. But I'd just spent the last six months sat in that flat on me own so if I wasn't gonna get yer to stay in, the least I was gonna get was a bit of drama before yer went out. Got more than I asked for.

RAY. Carla –

CARLA. So did you. Yer were white as a sheet. (*To* SIMON.) I'm sat there wipin' the blood out of me eyes and yer know what he says to me? Simon?

SIMON. No.

CARLA. 'Have yer got a field dressin'?'

Beat.

Honestly, 'have yer got a field dressin'?' Cos apparently if it don't bleed through one of them it don't need stitchin'. A fuckin' field dressin'. Funny enough I didn't. Don't think they sell 'em at the Boots in Frenchgate.

RAY. Stop it, Carla.

CARLA. I don't think I were expectin' yer to come home and sweep me off me feet like in *An Officer and a Gentleman*. But I didn't think I'd be sat in the kitchen holdin' a max-flow sanitary pad to me head either.

RAY. It ain't funny.

CARLA. I know that, Ray.

CARLA *lights a cigarette.* SIMON *looks at her disapprovingly.*

I will shove it up yer arse, Simon, I swear!

SIMON. Did I say anythin'?

Pause.

CARLA. Yer know what, Ray? At least yer stay true to yerself. Most blokes would of come in here tonight cryin' their hearts out and promisin' they'd change. You came in and threw the barmaid on the floor. Yer might as well of been wearin' one of them sandwich-board things that says, 'Just in case yer were wonderin', Carla, I'm still a fuckin' nightmare!'

Pause.

LEANNE. I feel sick.

Pause.

Really sick.

RAY. Drink through it.

LEANNE. I need to go.

RAY. No yer don't.

LEANNE. Me mum worries if she wakes up and I'm not home.

RAY. Yer a big girl, Leanne.

LEANNE. I'll need to go for a pee soon.

RAY. Then go.

LEANNE. Didn't think yer'd let me.

RAY. Why?

LEANNE. I might escape through the toilet window.

RAY. Trust me, if you can do the acrobatics needed to get through that little window, I'll fuck Carla off and take *you* to Brighton.

CARLA. And yer wonder why I'm not fallin' into yer arms.

SIMON. Look, Ray, this is nothin' to do with Leanne. Can't she just go?

CARLA. At last, it mans up!

SIMON. Ray?

RAY. No.

LEANNE. Why?

RAY. Cos the minute yer get out yer'll call the old bill.

LEANNE. I won't, I promise.

RAY. Promises from women mean shite. Carla promised 'till death do us part'. What I actually got were a court order to leave me own house and her weddin' ring sat on it like a fuckin' full stop.

LEANNE *looks upset*.

Yer not gonna cry are yer?

CARLA. That's scarier than the Taliban to you, ain't it, Ray, a cryin' woman?

RAY. Oh, come on. We're still havin' fun, ain't we? Thought yer wanted to hear about the Army. Thought yer wanted stuff to tell yer brother.

CARLA. She wanted to hear about passin' out parades and medals, Ray. But she's gettin' the real deal tonight. The stuff that ain't in the brochure.

RAY. What's that s'posed to mean?

CARLA. They come back in a box or off their box. Tell yer brother that.

RAY. Shut up, Carla.

CARLA. One lad he served with in Afghanistan slit his arm from elbow to wrist then stuck his fingers in and tore out a vein. Said he needed to pull his wires out.

LEANNE. What did he do that for?

CARLA. Cos he were fucked in the head. A bit like the bloke who's got us locked in a pub. Has it stopped bein' a giggle yet?

LEANNE *starts to cry*.

RAY. No don't cry. There's no need for that. Carla!

LEANNE. I wanna go home.

RAY. And yer can. In a bit.

Pause.

Yer know, I like yer, Leanne. Really I do.

CARLA. I think shaggin' her is prob'ly off the table now, Ray, don't you?

RAY. I mean I like her as a mate, Carla.

LEANNE. Yer got a funny way of showin' it.

RAY. I'm sorry for pushin' yer. I shouldn't of done that. I get wound up. I can't think straight. But I don't want yer to go. I want yer to stay so we can talk more.

CARLA. Jesus, Ray, ain't yer got a Transit van to go to tonight?

Something appears to snap in RAY. *He looks for a second like he might go for* CARLA.

RAY. Yer know, if yer don't stop talkin' I don't know what I'll do. Will yer just for one minute stop talkin'?

CARLA *is frightened.*

CARLA. Okay, Ray. I'm sorry.

SIMON. It's alright, Ray. Let's everyone just calm down a bit.

RAY. I'm perfectly calm when she ain't in me ear.

Silence.

RAY *pours himself a drink and one for* LEANNE. *He hands it to her.*

Peace offerin'.

LEANNE *takes the drink and sips a little.*

Yer got some balls, you, ain't yer? The way yer were gonna go for that key earlier. Yer brother got balls like you?

LEANNE. Dunno.

RAY. Well, I reckon the British Army'll be alright if he does.

LEANNE *smiles weakly.*

That's better. Yer know much about the war in Afghanistan, do yer?

LEANNE. Not really.

RAY. Why yer so keen for him to fight in it then?

LEANNE. Dunno.

RAY. Yer must have some idea.

LEANNE. Me old man always says it's that or prison for him. I used to think he fancied himself as a bit of a fortune-teller. Now I think he's just givin' him his choices. When yer think about it, he's right. What else is there round here?

Pause.

Me dad says some blokes are born to have letters after their name and some numbers. They should hand 'em out at birth, save confusion.

RAY. Yer dad in the Army was he?

LEANNE. Nah. He worked the pit at Barnsley and it did his chest in. He were like an old man by the time he were forty. Always kicked himself for it. Said the lads comin' back from the Falklands got old dears' kisses and young girls' knickers and the poor old miners got it all arse about face.

RAY. They're reasons, I s'pose.

LEANNE. I used to tell me friends he were dead. That the bloke at the school gate were me granddad. He would've been a rubbish soldier anyway. Wouldn't say boo to a goose.

RAY. It ain't for everyone. Not everyone can live on their nerves. It ain't a war how yer'd imagine it. Yer not fightin' soldiers in uniform. They're peasants. Everyone looks the same. Yer don't know who the enemy is till they shoot at yer.

LEANNE. Then how d'yer know when yer've killed 'em all?

RAY. Yer don't. But yer know yer never will anyway cos for every one yer kill, yer make another. Sometimes more than one. It's like a fuckin' zombie film.

LEANNE. How d'yer mean?

RAY. That bloke yer just killed. Their dad or their brother or their son. He might of been a farmer beforehand but by the time he's scooped his lad off the road, he ain't any more.

Pause.

We came across this kid once in Sangin. A little kid. He were in a field at the side of the road. He were cryin' and callin' to us. So me mate starts across the field to get to him, the second one of us follows. I would've followed too but suddenly I know what's gonna happen before it even does and I try to call out but it's too late. I'm on me back and there's shit rainin' down on me. I open me eyes and sit up and I already know what I'm gonna see, me mates in bits. But they're not, they're just pickin' 'emselves up the same as me. The kid must of fucked up the timin' or the device has just gone off on its own or somethin'. But he's just lyin' there with his guts flopped out next to him. Shiny like tar cos blood looks black in the dark. He ain't even managed to kill himself. He's just lyin' there, gaspin' his last, lookin' up at the three blokes he's just tried to off.

Pause.

LEANNE. Jesus.

SIMON. I'm goin' for a slash.

CARLA. Simon!

SIMON. What? I need to pee and I've heard it before.

Exit SIMON.

LEANNE *goes to the bar to get another drink.*

CARLA. I don't like it when yer tell that story. I don't like to think of yer goin' through it again.

RAY. I only got through it cos I knew what were waitin' at the end.

CARLA. Don't, Ray.

RAY. You and the kids. Me angels.

CARLA. Please don't do this.

RAY. I used to close me eyes and see yer bathin' 'em. Them all soft and pink and wrinkled and yer clothes soaked through. I could smell the baby oil on their skin and it were like it were cleanin' me of all the dirtiness and ugliness I'd seen.

CARLA *touches his face.*

CARLA. Shhh.

RAY. And everythin' made sense cos I were makin' the world safer for you and them. I were yer protector. I were yer lion.

CARLA *smiles*.

Yer remember Warren sayin' that? 'Yer a lion, Daddy.' I could've cried with happiness.

CARLA. Only now yer a wounded lion, ain't yer, Ray?

RAY. Pathetic.

CARLA. Dangerous.

RAY. Please come with me, Carla. I can get sorted if yer with me. I'd have a reason to.

CARLA. If it were just about me then maybe, Ray. But what about the boys? I'm not draggin' them halfway across the country so they can watch yer drink and fight yerself to death and prob'ly half batter me in the process.

RAY. I can't stay here. I can't go to prison.

SIMON *returns. He sees* CARLA *touching* RAY*'s face.* CARLA *notices* SIMON *and moves her hand.*

CARLA. Yer angels were never a good enough reason to stay, were they? Even when yer friends were home with their babies, yer'd rather be out wanderin' the streets on yer own. But never alone for long cos in good old Donny there's always a stranger to get pissed with or fight with or fuck.

RAY. I never cheated.

CARLA. Don't make a liar of yerself.

Pause.

It were almost a relief when yer stopped bein' interested in me. Cos for months beforehand yer wouldn't come near me unless yer were drunk and even then yer fucked me like yer hated me.

RAY. I never hated yer, Carla. I hated me life. I came back and it felt like it didn't fit me prop'ly. Like I'd grown out of it.

CARLA. Like yer'd grown out of me.

RAY. I've seen people whose whole lives are about tryin' to put food in their gobs and tryin' not to get blown up or bent double screamin' at the graves of folk who *did* get blown up. How d'yer go from that to watchin' *X Factor* with a plate of Chinese on yer knee? How d'yer do that month after fuckin' month until yer old and pissin' yerself in a home? Waitin' for a visit that never comes from the brats yer worshipped like gods.

Pause.

How d'yer face the thought of dyin' when yer never fuckin' lived?

CARLA. Most of us don't need to feel threatened to feel like we're livin'. That is livin' for most people, Ray. TV, takeaway and the kids. It's enough.

RAY. Then why are yer here? Pissed up in the middle of the week with yer kids dumped on someone else. Because yer bored, Carla.

CARLA. Yer know I start to feel sorry for yer and then yer remind me what an arsehole yer are.

RAY. I'm not gettin' at yer. I'm askin' yer.

CARLA. Sometimes I do get bored, Ray. But not cos me life is easy. I get bored of the struggle. I get bored of talkin' to kids. I get bored of workin' two jobs so we can have that Chinese at the weekend. If I made it look easy that's cos I were scared yer'd stop comin' back, not cos there were ever a day when it weren't a struggle.

RAY. I'm an idiot, Carla. Yer the one bit of good luck I've ever had and I lost sight of it. Let all this shit fill me head.

Pause.

I have this dream about bringin' yer locket to yer. It's the only important thing gettin' this locket to yer. I'm wadin' through water with me fist clenched above me head. But when I open me fist, d'yer know what's there?

CARLA. No.

RAY. Fuck-all, Carla. Me palm is full of nail marks, that's all. And I'm cryin' when I tell yer cos I know how much it means to yer and how upset yer'll be it's gone. But yer know what yer say when I tell yer?

CARLA. No.

RAY. Yer say, 'Ray sweetheart, I don't own a locket.'

CARLA. Well, I don't.

RAY. I know that. That's not the point.

CARLA. Well, what is the point then?

RAY. I dunno.

LEANNE. I used to have a dream that I would go out of the house, get all the way to school then notice I hadn't put any knickers or a skirt on. What d'yer think that means?

SIMON. It either means yer very forgetful or yer a slut.

LEANNE. That's charmin', that is!

SIMON. Yeah well, charming's for idiots I reckon. When I were young I used to tell girls I liked that I'd had dreams about fuckin' 'em.

RAY. What?

SIMON. I think I thought it were better than just tellin' 'em I wanted to fuck 'em.

RAY. I have no idea what yer talkin' about.

SIMON. I'm talkin' about makin' up dreams that yer never had cos it's easier than just sayin' what yer want to say. I should've just told the truth. I'd of spent more time fuckin' and less time talkin' about dreams.

CARLA. Are yer pissed, Simon?

SIMON. Would yer like me to be?

RAY. You sayin' I made me dream up?

SIMON. People treat dreams like they mean somethin' when really they mean fuck-all.

RAY. Yer sayin' I'm a liar, Simon?

SIMON. *Are* yer a liar, Ray?

CARLA. It don't matter.

RAY. Matters to me. (*Prepares to fight with* SIMON.) Come on then, right now!

CARLA. Ray, yer need to stop this! I could slap yer silly I really could and I could cry me heart out for yer at the same time. Yer need to let someone help yer.

Silence.

RAY. I bet yer a shot of vodka that none of yer know how many soldiers have died in Afghanistan.

RAY *pours a shot of vodka.*

Do you know, Carla?

CARLA. No.

RAY. That's a shot for you then.

CARLA. Don't be stupid, Ray.

RAY. I'll drink it for yer.

He downs the shot and pours another.

What about you, Leanne. Do you know?

LEANNE. No.

RAY. Yer'd better drink that then.

LEANNE. I'll puke.

RAY. Suit yerself.

RAY *downs the shot and pours another.*

Come on then, Simon. Let's see if you know.

SIMON. I don't, Ray.

RAY. C'mon, have a stab. Are we talkin' one hundred? Three hundred?

SIMON. I dunno.

RAY. Yer don't know and yer don't care. I won't even ask yer to down yours, yer faggot.

RAY *downs the shot. Pours another.*

Now the funny thing is yer prob'ly all think I know. But I don't so that's a shot for me too.

RAY *downs a shot.*

Yer see I'd never really thought about it till today. They showed three more bodies comin' back on the news. They had it on in the pub with the sound down. I only noticed it by chance and when I looked around me I saw that no one else had or they had and they didn't care. They were all drinkin' and laughin' and chattin'. But I can't take me eyes off it. The sight of 'em marchin' makes me throat ache, it always does. I used to think it were pride but now I ain't sure. It shouldn't hurt yer, should it, pride? So I'm watchin' and achin' and then suddenly, there's Gerrard puttin' one over the crossbar. Someone's gone and fuckin' switched channel. Takes me a second to work out who but then I spot him down the outside of the bar, this Asian lad. He puts the remote down and turns back to the bloke he's talkin' to. I shout to him, 'I were watchin' that,' and yer know what he says?

Pause.

'No one else looks too bothered, mate.' So I ask him if he knows how many British soldiers have died in Afghanistan and he says, 'Go on then, mate, enlighten me.'

Beat.

If I could've enlightened him he might still be walkin' now.

Pause.

SIMON. Does it worry yer that none of it means anythin', Ray?

RAY. Yer what?

SIMON. Does it worry yer that maybe yer beat up a bloke just cos he didn't pretend to give a shit like everyone else does?

CARLA. What yer talkin' about?

SIMON. Yer know, some of them blokes bein' brought back in boxes will have been shot with guns that we gave to the Afghans when they were on our side. How can it mean anythin' if we can change sides? What if we're not really fightin' for anythin'? What if we're just fightin' cos that's what we do?

LEANNE. That's just daft, Simon. Them blokes are out there fightin' for us. To keep us all safe from terrorists. They're heroes.

SIMON. I'm just sayin'.

CARLA. Well, don't. Leanne's right, have a bit of respect.

SIMON. And what am I respectin' exactly, Carla? The bloke who just beat someone up for changin' the channel?

CARLA. He didn't beat anyone up for changin' the channel, Simon. He beat him up over a principle.

SIMON. I've seen a lot of pub fights in me time, Carla, and not many of 'em were over a principle. Some were about anger or about loss of face and some were even about greed. And it might of been principles sweatin' through the skin of the blokes throwin' punches but it stank a lot like booze.

CARLA. You okay, Ray? Yer very quiet?

Beat.

Ray?

RAY. Sometimes I sit on the banks of the Don at night and I can hear the blokes in the prison shoutin' to each other. Sounds like barracks.

CARLA. I could bring the kids to see yer there, Ray. It wouldn't be for ever. Not like if yer run to Brighton.

RAY. Yer'd really bring 'em?

CARLA. I promise.

RAY. I'd like that.

SIMON. Yer can tell the court yer a hero, Ray. They might take it into account how hard it were for yer seein' that kid blown up. Not much older than Jamie.

CARLA. Simon's right. They'll prob'ly feel sorry for yer.

SIMON. I mean, don't tell 'em yer pissed on him, like.

CARLA. What?

RAY. You bastard.

SIMON. Oh, were that a secret?

CARLA. What are yer talkin' about, Simon?

SIMON. Ray pissed on that kid, Carla. As he lay dyin'. He told me. One night when we were here. When he were drunk.

CARLA. Why would yer say somethin' so nasty?

SIMON. Cos it's true. Yer opened yer trousers, didn't yer, Ray, and pissed on him. In his mouth and his eyes and his gapin' fuckin' guts.

CARLA. No yer didn't, did yer, Ray?

Beat.

Ray?

RAY. All of us did.

SIMON. But you first. Yer saw a child dyin' on the ground and yer first thought were to piss on him.

LEANNE. Jesus.

RAY. Stop sayin' it.

SIMON. It's hard to understand.

RAY. For you.

SIMON. For all of us, Ray.

RAY *looks around him at the incomprehension on their faces.*

RAY. Yer ever felt yer arse go, Simon?

SIMON. Dunno what yer mean.

RAY. It's like it flutters or somethin'. When yer know yer in real trouble.

Beat.

They don't mention it in the movies. Don't s'pose it sounds right in a war film, does it? 'Me arse is goin' like a bag of butterflies.' But that's how it goes. Yer ain't felt that – yer ain't been scared. Not really.

SIMON. Why are yer tellin' me that?

RAY. Yer think yer can judge me? Yer not even a man. Yer a tissue full of spunk that someone left on the radiator to grow.

SIMON. Says you.

RAY. Yer want puttin' out of yer fuckin' misery.

SIMON. How long before yer kids start tellin' their friends yer dead, Ray, and yer just become the rabid fuckin' stray that's always sniffin' round their mum?

RAY *pushes* SIMON *backwards. He crashes into the table and ends up on the floor.* RAY *stands over* SIMON. *He grabs a bottle of vodka and douses him in it.*

What the fuck are yer doin'?

CARLA. Ray, stop it!

RAY *takes out his matches and lights one. He holds it above* SIMON. SIMON *screams in panic.*

SIMON. Jesus, Ray!

CARLA. Ray!

RAY. Is yer arse goin' now, is it?

SIMON. I'm sorry! Ray!

RAY *drops the match. It lands on* SIMON *and goes out.* RAY *bursts into laughter.*

RAY. Two parts fuckin' water. Your fuckin' face.

SIMON *struggles but* RAY *doesn't let him up.*

The thing about fear is the moment yer show it is the moment it's beaten yer.

RAY *lets* SIMON *up.*

SIMON. You fuckin' areshole. Yer think yer the only one who knows anythin' about fear? Yer think I haven't spent months worryin' what yer gonna do when yer find out about me and Carla? I have. But *I've* never forgotten that she's the best bit of luck I've ever had. That's the difference between us.

RAY. It's not the only one by a long shot.

SIMON. And yer think she's not scared, Ray? Yer think she don't worry about puttin' food on the table and the shitty streets her kids are runnin' about on with junkies on every fuckin' corner? Cos you're not gonna worry about that, are yer? Some of us don't need to go to the desert to find out what fear is.

Pause.

But then, I'm not sure you did either.

RAY. Is that right?

SIMON. I think yer've been scared yer whole life, Ray. As long as I've known yer anyway. Yer stick yer chest out and yer throw yer weight about and yer hope no one sees it. Must of been like all yer Christmasses come at once the day someone offered yer a uniform and a pay packet to do it.

RAY. Yer see, I wouldn't expect a pathetic little squat-thrust like you to know what it is to fight for yer country.

SIMON. I don't, Ray. I don't understand what it means or why it's worth spillin' one drop of blood over. Just looks like a big old pub fight to me.

Pause.

It were me who took yer photo down. It made me sick to the stomach just lookin' at it. You make me sick, Ray, d'yer know that?

Pause.

Yer've travelled halfway across the world and all yer've learnt is that yer were right to shit yerself. The world is a fuckin' scary place, where kids blow 'emselves up and grown men go mad and people who yer thought would love yer for ever just stop one day. And the worst thing is no one gives a shit about any of it. But yer don't do fear, do yer, Ray? Better to try and make the stuff that scares yer disappear.

RAY. Yer don't know what the fuck yer talkin' about.

SIMON. Yer piss on a kid and yer make him an animal – (*Taps his head.*) in here at least. Yer pour enough vodka down yer throat and yer can't feel a thing.

RAY. That's true enough.

SIMON. Yer lock the door and nobody can leave yer, can they?

RAY. Shut yer mouth.

SIMON. But it's all bollocks, Ray, cos a pissed-on child is still a child and a fucked-up drunk is still fucked up when he's sober. Yer see, I don't think fear has beaten yer just cos yer let it show. I don't think it's beaten yer till it's pullin' yer strings. And yer fuckin' dancin', ain't yer?

SIMON takes the key from the bar and unlocks the door.

Do what yer want, Ray, but I'm not sittin' here all night.

Pause.

RAY. I think that's the most faggotty thing I've ever heard yer say and that's sayin' somethin'.

SIMON. C'mon, Leanne. Yer need to go home. Leanne!

LEANNE has her head on the table. She sits up.

LEANNE. What?

SIMON. Home.

LEANNE checks the time.

LEANNE. I can't go home at this time. Me mum'll batter me.

SIMON. And what'll she do if yer don't go home at all?

LEANNE. She'll still batter me but at least it'll be tomorrow.

SIMON. Suit yerself. (*To* CARLA.) I'm gonna tidy up then I'm goin' to bed.

SIMON starts to clear glasses.

Silence other than the clinking of glasses, etc.

CARLA. Did yer do that, did yer, Ray? Did yer piss on that child?

RAY looks at CARLA.

RAY. Yer'll never guess what?

CARLA. What?

RAY. I just lost the game.

RAY pours a vodka and downs it. He pours another.

And again.

He downs it and pours another.

And again.

RAY *downs the vodka. He goes to pour another but it is empty.*

I can't get drunk on this. I can't even drink meself to death.

RAY *angrily knocks some of the glasses from the table. Then he starts to cry.* SIMON *stops what he is doing.* LEANNE *sits up.*

CARLA. Come on, Ray. There's no need for that.

LEANNE. Jesus, it's like seein' yer dad cry. It's weird.

CARLA. Shut up, Leanne.

RAY (*still crying*). Yer look at me like yer hate me and I can't stand it. I wanna rip yer eyes out and crush 'em in me hands.

CARLA. I don't hate yer, Ray. I don't have the energy.

RAY (*stops crying*). Don't say me name.

CARLA. What?

RAY. Yer say me name and it sounds like a swear word. Honestly, yer say it and I wish I were called anythin' else.

CARLA. Who do yer want to be then, Ray? David, Tony, who?

RAY. I told yer, anyone. Someone yer like.

CARLA. I like *you*.

CARLA *hugs* RAY. *He lets her but he doesn't reciprocate.*

RAY. I know a guy who lost his legs in Afghanistan. They gave him bionic ones and now he runs marathons. I dunno what I lost out there but I don't think they can give it me back.

CARLA. Shhhh.

SIMON. I'm tired, Carla. I'm goin' to bed.

Pause.

You comin'?

Pause.

Carla?

CARLA. How can I, Simon? Yer want me to just leave him down here like this?

SIMON. No, I want him to fuck off out of me pub.

CARLA. Shall we just chuck him out onto the street then?

SIMON. He ain't our problem.

CARLA. No, Simon, he ain't *your* problem.

SIMON. Yer a sucker for a wounded soldier, ain't yer?

CARLA. He's me husband.

SIMON. He's yer ex-husband. It's only two letters and they're gettin' fuckin' smaller by the minute.

CARLA. I'm not just chuckin' him out. He'll have to come to mine if he can't stay here.

SIMON. Suit yerself, I'm goin' to bed.

CARLA. I'll call yer when I get home.

SIMON. Don't bother.

CARLA. I'll phone yer tomorrow then.

SIMON. I don't want yer to.

CARLA. Don't be like that.

SIMON. Like what, Carla?

CARLA. Cold. It ain't like yer.

SIMON. Yeah well, I'm sick of bein' like me. Bein' like me don't get yer nowhere.

CARLA. That ain't true. Why are yer sayin' that?

SIMON. Yer got about a million reasons for not bein' with him, Carla, and not one of 'em is me. I dunno why I'm surprised. Yer know the only time a bloke like me gets a girl like you, Carla? When yer fed up of bein' bounced off walls by blokes like him. But we know deep down it's only a borrow. Cos when the bruises fade yer go runnin' back to 'em like bitches on heat.

CARLA. Simon!

SIMON. I'm sorry. Yer not used to hearin' me talk like that, are yer? I could give yer a fat lip and all. Make it really feel like home.

Pause.

Yer said earlier that yer didn't love him, that it were the opposite, yer hated him. I do think yer hate him but it ain't the opposite to love cos that's not givin' a shit, Carla, and you still do. I think this is what love turns into and yer know what? It's very fuckin' ugly and yer welcome to it.

CARLA. I'm sorry, Simon.

SIMON. For what? Yer can't make yerself love someone if yer don't. And yer don't, do yer?

Pause.

RAY. I'd take that as a no if I were you.

SIMON. Shut up.

Pause.

Do yer, Carla?

CARLA. I'm sorry.

SIMON *exits*.

Pause.

RAY. I really think he might be gay, Carla.

CARLA. Oh, just shut up, Ray.

RAY. Well –

CARLA. Just shut up. Bein' with him were the closest I've come to livin' in a long time.

RAY. But yer don't love him.

CARLA. Yeah well, love can be a right pain in the arse if yer ask me, Ray. It's just a fuckin' brick I carry round with me.

RAY. Don't say that.

CARLA. Come on.

RAY. What?

CARLA. We'll have to walk back to mine. I can't call us a taxi cos it'd prob'ly end up bein' an Asian and yer'd feel the need to beat the shit out of him. Yer know, I'd be better off if yer had got yer legs blown off in Afghanistan.

RAY. That's nice that is.

CARLA. No really, people would get that. They'd say, 'Look at that poor cow pullin' him in and out of his wheelchair. She's a fuckin' saint.' Yer don't get any Brownie points for babysittin' a fuckin' psycho.

RAY. I ain't comin' with yer.

CARLA. Don't be daft, Ray. I didn't mean it.

RAY. I'm serious and not cos of what yer just said.

CARLA. Where yer gonna go? Brighton?

RAY. No.

CARLA. Well, where then?

RAY. That ain't your problem.

CARLA. Course it is.

RAY. Well, I don't want it to be.

Pause.

I want to be a lion, Carla. In the boys' eyes if nothin' else.

CARLA. Yer just bein' stupid, Ray.

RAY. Promise me yer won't tell 'em where I am.

CARLA. Ray –

RAY. Promise me yer won't bring 'em to visit.

RAY *grabs* CARLA *roughly.*

Are yer listenin' to me?

CARLA. Yes.

RAY. Do yer promise?

CARLA. Yes.

RAY. Yer can't break a promise. Not again.

CARLA. Yer hurtin' me, Ray.

Pause.

RAY. I know.

RAY *lets go of* CARLA.

Go upstairs.

CARLA. What?

RAY. Go upstairs and speak to Simon.

CARLA. Why, Ray?

RAY. Go and make it right. Yer need yer mates, Carla.

CARLA. I don't think he needs mates like me.

RAY. I reckon he'll have yer in his life in any way he can.

RAY *puts his T-shirt on.*

Anyway, yer shouldn't be wanderin' around out there at this time of night. There's all kinds of weirdos.

CARLA *stares at* RAY*'s bloody T-shirt. He looks down and sees the irony.*

CARLA *looks at* LEANNE, *who is head-down on the table again.*

CARLA. What about her?

RAY. Well, she's a bit odd but I wouldn't of called her a weirdo.

CARLA. Yer know what I mean.

RAY. Let her sleep. She's gonna have a headache to kill a civvy in the mornin'. She shouldn't drink like that if she can't handle it.

CARLA. Yer sure yer gonna be alright?

RAY. I'm sure.

Pause.

CARLA. I'll see yer then, Ray.

RAY. Yeah.

CARLA hesitates.

Go.

CARLA exits.

RAY drains a couple of the vodka glasses on the table.

He goes over to LEANNE and watches her sleeping.

Yer actually not much better lookin' than Denise.

LEANNE. I'm awake.

She sits up.

RAY. Yeah I knew that. Had yer goin' though, didn't I?

Beat.

Well, I'm off now. It were good to meet yer. Sorry about everythin'.

LEANNE. It's alright. I'm not gonna tell the police or nothin'.

RAY. Okay. Thanks.

RAY goes to the door and takes the key out of the lock.

Tell yer brother though, won't yer?

LEANNE nods.

RAY exits and closes the door behind him before locking the door from the outside and posting the key back through the letterbox.

Lights down.

A Nick Hern Book

Glory Dazed first published in Great Britain as a paperback original in 2013 by Nick Hern Books Limited, The Glasshouse, 49a Goldhawk Road, London W12 8QP, in association with Second Shot Productions and Soho Theatre

Glory Dazed copyright © 2013 Cat Jones

Cat Jones has asserted her right to be identified as the author of this work

Cover photograph: *Glory Dazed*, Old Vic New Voices Edinburgh Season 2012, Alex Brenner
Cover design: Ned Hoste, 2H

Typeset by Nick Hern Books
Printed in Great Britain by Mimeo Ltd, St Ives, Cambs, PE27 3LE

A CIP catalogue record for this book is available from the British Library

ISBN   978 1 84842 323 7